STOPGAP

WINNIPEG

STOPGAP

Liam Card

DUNDURN
TORONTO

Copyright © Liam Card, 2016

All rights reserved. No part of this publication may be reproduced, stored in a retrieval system, or transmitted in any form or by any means, electronic, mechanical, photocopying, recording, or otherwise (except for brief passages for purpose of review) without the prior permission of Dundurn Press. Permission to photocopy should be requested from Access Copyright.

Project editor: Shannon Whibbs
Editor: Allister Thompson
Cover designer: Laura Boyle
Interior design: Courtney Horner
Cover image: Background: © selimaksan/istockphoto.com, Man & Hand: © Michael Brown/123RF
Printer: Webcom

Library and Archives Canada Cataloguing in Publication

Card, Liam, 1980-, author
    Stopgap / Liam Card.

Issued in print and electronic formats.
ISBN 978-1-4597-3292-6 (paperback).--ISBN 978-1-4597-3293-3 (pdf).--
ISBN 978-1-4597-3294-0 (epub)

    I. Title.

PS8605.A688S76 2016   C813'.6   C2015-904376-X
                                                  C2015-904377-8

1 2 3 4 5   20 19 18 17 16

We acknowledge the support of the **Canada Council for the Arts** and the **Ontario Arts Council** for our publishing program. We also acknowledge the financial support of the **Government of Canada** through the **Canada Book Fund** and **Livres Canada Books**, and the **Government of Ontario** through the **Ontario Book Publishing Tax Credit** and the **Ontario Media Development Corporation**.

Care has been taken to trace the ownership of copyright material used in this book. The author and the publisher welcome any information enabling them to rectify any references or credits in subsequent editions.

— *J. Kirk Howard, President*

The publisher is not responsible for websites or their content unless they are owned by the publisher.

Printed and bound in Canada.

VISIT US AT
Dundurn.com | @dundurnpress | Facebook.com/dundurnpress | Pinterest.com/dundurnpress

Dundurn
3 Church Street, Suite 500
Toronto, Ontario, Canada
M5E 1M2

For Kelda

1

For much of my abbreviated life on Earth, the relationship I had with death was as inconsistent as it was mystifying. As a boy, attempting to wrap my mind around the unflinching laws of nature seemed the most unnatural of tasks — a mental decathlon resulting in total upheaval versus that of order and balance. Suddenly, life no longer came with a guarantee on the packaging. Life was something that could be lost. And not lost like an action figure or a baseball over the fence. Not like a scarf or rogue winter glove that could find its way into the lost and found. Life was now something that could be permanently unaccounted for. No tricky coin slot for second tries. No chairlift up for another wild run at it. On any given day, one could happen to be without it.

Dead.

Suddenly, everyone and everything around me had an ambiguous expiration date. There we were, risking our lives at every turn. What used to be an enjoyable car ride to soccer or a movie was now a harrowing game of Russian Roulette. Visits with pals became a process of in-depth risk analysis. "Luke, would you like to play with James today?" Not a chance I'm risking my one lap around

the track to see that guy. Though, remarkably, certain things qualified — people, places, and events that were worth climbing into an
assembly of moving parts and flammable liquids to visit. I would sit
in the back seat of Dad's Chevy Parisienne and cross my fingers with
each passing car, holding my breath as transport trucks screamed
past me. Dad would tell me it was fine. He would say that the big
boat was as safe as anything they sent into space. But I'd heard that
from time to time space shuttles exploded, and, even at that age, I
knew those things cost more than Dad's Parisienne.

Just another lie to calm the young mind.

Previous to becoming a member of those in the know, past
promises surrounding the issue of death revealed themselves to
be nothing more than an inside joke. Preceding any knowledge
of death, the snake on the road being worked into the pavement
with the rubber of each passing car was just sleeping. As was the
neighbours' German shepherd, the bloated carcass of which was
carried out of the ditch with a snow shovel.

He was just taking a nap.

As was the deer strewn across the highway.

As was the snail smeared across the sidewalk with its mobile
home in a million tiny pieces.

He looks hurt, I'd say.

No, he'll pull himself together when he wakes up.

That's how it works. That's what we're promised as children.

Then one day that promise dies and is shipped to the graveyard
of untruths.

For most, the introduction to death becomes inescapable when a
loved one has passed. Here, the word *died* or *dead* is first used and is
then explained with hushed tones, back rubs, and comforting hugs.
We voice that our stomach is in knots and our heart is breaking over
this confusing news, this concept, this introduction to endings, until,
rest assured, that recently deceased loved one, along with the entire
collection of missing family pets, have all gone to a better place.

A better place above the clouds to be with God.

A place called Heaven.

We're fed these new promises for pain relief, like Tylenol. Then we all feel better for a while, until the next heartache. Then more Tylenol. Life is never the same when our youthful minds are directed to meet Death. After we are forced to acknowledge his presence. Bent with confusion, we're asked to outstretch our trembling right arm, open our clenched fist, and shake the giant black tarantula he boasts for a hand.

Pleasure to meet you, Death.

We pull over our adventurous voyage with Life and unwittingly invite Death to ride along for the remainder of our journey. Life sits in the front, passenger side. Death sits in the back, chauffeured, and without the requirement for any shallow banter. He just sits there patiently observing our fascinating interaction with Life.

Thrilled to be present is Death — and only ever a glance away in the rearview mirror in case you forget he's there. Which, of course, happens from time to time. We tend to get caught up in our roaring relationship with Life and stop checking our rearview mirror. We do wild, outrageous, careless things with Life, and then it's too late. Death taps us on the shoulder from behind the driver's seat with his grotesquely long spider-leg finger, awkwardly hinges open his broken jaw, and whispers, "Remember me?"

Yes, he's been there the whole time.

Ready to receive us.

Loyal to a fault is Death. Certainly far more loyal than Life. Life is fickle. It can leave you at a moment's notice. Life can terminate a beautiful relationship in mere seconds and without the slightest trace of remorse. Life will desert you for the love or abuse of it; for the care taken along the way or the complete lack thereof.

It doesn't matter.

Sooner or later, Life reveals its true colours, its despicable fair-weather tendencies.

· · ·

It was Granddad Stevenson who forced my introduction to Death. He was in the process of teaching me how to play chess when he told me I could only count on two things in life: death and taxes. He had a million sayings like that one. I was quite young when he dropped that gem on me. Five, I think.

"What's taxes?" I said.

"When you make money, you always have to give some back."

"To who?"

"To the country. To the government."

"Why?"

"Now there's a good goddamn question worth asking! I should give you a loudspeaker and set you up on Parliament Hill." He laughed hard. Then he snorted and broke into a chunky coughing fit. He'd bang at his chest with a closed fist and tell me the old speakers were popping in there. He'd swirl his drink so that the ice cubes knocked shoulders a few times before it went down the hatch.

"What's death?" I said.

"Jesus Christ," he said and rearranged the wisps of hair populating the top of his freckled head.

From there, this decorated veteran of war explained the concept of death with the utmost colour and candour, as one who had witnessed death of all kinds would do. With regard to his explanation of death, this is what he finished with: "So just get used to it."

"That's not true," I said.

"Luke, when your dad and I stuffed poor Apple Basket into the wood stove, did you really think it was because he was cold?" he said, breathing old coffee and new whisky on me. "The poor little bastard was dead."

Apple Basket was an orange tabby I used to carry around in an apple basket when he was a kitten. To this day, no one knows where Apple Basket came from. Mom was out hanging laundry on the line, and when she reached down to pick out more bedding, there was the kitten, kneading the dirty bedsheets with his front paws and purring like a hedge trimmer. When Mom came back in from the line, she dropped the basket in front of Dad and me. She placed her hands, thumbs forward on her hips, and said, "We now have a cat. This is his home. That is his bedding. This is a sign from God. I need a proper laundry basket."

And that was that.

Apple Basket was mine, and Mom bought herself a brand-new wicker laundry basket. The kitten and his new home of the same name lived on the floor at the foot of my bed. After a few months, and some growth, he would make his way out of the basket and would fashion a nest in the duvet cover between my feet. This little guy was my best pal in the whole world. With a piece of string dangling from a twig, he would entertain me with a circus lineup of backflips, mid-air swats, and feats of athleticism for hours on end. Over time, Apple Basket became increasingly adventurous. Sadly, the twig-and-string routine began to bore him, and his wild eyes told me that he was ready for bigger and better things. Something with a heartbeat. Something with wings. Something with whiskers and a tail. Training camp was over, and he was ready to turn pro.

Every deadly sniper relies on a trusted spotter, but in the hunt I was more a hindrance than a help to Apple Basket. He would turn and look back, as if begging me to not follow him into battle. We eventually agreed that he could have the afternoons to himself, and he was pleased with that. I knew this because he would bring his trophies home to me and lay them dead centre on the doormat. He would sit majestically alongside whatever was now baking in the hot summer sun until I came home and gave him applause. He would circle me a dozen times, snaking his tail around my calves. Mom would promptly collect the prize and take it away. The bird or mouse had lost the fight, and she was taking it somewhere to heal before it could battle once again.

Apple Basket never lost a fight.

Until he did.

One afternoon I came home and there was no trophy waiting for me. No Apple Basket either. A few days passed, and Mom and I stapled pictures of him with our phone number on them to telephone poles around the neighbourhood. Eventually, Dad found him on the side of the road and said he was badly hurt and extremely cold. Being so severely hurt and cold meant that my best pal in the whole world required warming up inside the old wood stove before he could depart on a great adventure.

This adventure was his duty, I was told. His calling from the great cat lord, King Lionel.

I became sick with the news and asked if I could go into the wood stove — if I could go on the adventure. But it was explained to me that it was a magical stove, only for burning wood and heating cats before they embark on great quests.

And that was the promise.

That was gospel.

I was fed that story for unbearable pain relief, like morphine.

. . .

After the chat with Granddad Stevenson, so began my obsession with death.

The million and one implications.

The uncertainty of it all — or did it all just go black? What was the point of an ant, especially when that ant is stepped on and spins around in circles, mortally wounded, until he's stepped on again to be finished? These were questions I would later learn humankind had been pondering since we could sharpen a flint.

"Are we all just spinning around waiting to be put out of our misery?" I said to Granddad Stevenson. He laughed so hard that I could see all of the silver puddles in his back teeth.

"I like that one a lot. Yes. My answer is yes. But listen to me, pal. We're to have as much fun as possible before the final squish. Understand?"

From that point, it became a self-imposed requirement to learn more about death. After dinner, I would position myself next to my father on the couch to watch the news. All kinds of death and suffering were reported there. News anchors with nice teeth and perfect hair spoke of death without the slightest emotion, as if robotic, as if stripped of humanity or any semblance of emotional quotient. Night after night, images of dead bodies from around the globe entered our home. People I'd never met. People with families and stories. People who used to smile and laugh and have friends, now bloodied, limp, and lifeless.

Something to be collected and discarded.

Their images were magically beamed into my little living room in Oakville so my father could shake his head and say, "What a damn shame," and then yell to my mother about how pissed off he was that the car had picked up another nail.

"Can't we do anything?" I'd ask.

"You're going to see the world tear itself apart ten times over, and there's nothing you can do."

This is what I would do:

I'd go up into my room every night after the news and crack the spine of a novel. I'd dive into worlds where people were saved and heroes won. It was my only respite from the awful, unpredictable place that was the world around me — an escapee living vicariously through the heroes of great fiction.

I slayed dragons. Saved empires. Restored order.

Protected everything from castles to kings and queens, common people to golden rings and sometimes, on occasion, I'd offer a ring to a maiden I had saved or won the heart of somewhere along the way. This is where I preferred to live.

I walked the hallways of elementary and high school relatively anonymous. Not a soul was aware of the heroic things I was doing between the hours of dinner and midnight. Such is the plight of the protagonist at times — acts of valour without recognition or reward. It didn't matter much. This was my alternate universe, and I largely preferred it to the one I was living in.

. . .

While my preteen and teenage years were consumed with wrapping my head around the implications surrounding death, devouring news, stacking my bookshelf, and coping with my inability to gain the interest of the opposite sex, I managed to shed the albatross of virginity during my first year at college.

Her name was Diana.

I didn't know her last name.

Not that I forgot it. It has more to do with the fact that the information was never shared with me. Frosh week: I was downing skunky keg beer out of a red plastic cup I had paid five dollars for. The alpha-looking gent with whom I had transacted for the cup assured me that I was paying for the cup, and the beer was free. He made a real point of that. You know, to get around the liquor laws.

"I'm just not sure that would hold up in court," I said.

"How about you buy the plastic cup or fuck off," he said.

I promptly bought the cup.

So did my roommate, Russell Stern, who had dragged me to the frosh party in the first place.

Russell wasn't all that handsome, but anything he lacked in looks, he made up for with gobs of wit and a boatload of confidence. The guy oozed it. Fearless when it came to successfully breaking ice. Undaunted by the prospect of rejection. Russell made a beeline for the prettiest girl at the party and struck up a conversation as easy as a match meets striking paper. A dozen or so feet away, I stood in absolute wonderment. He seemed to be able to make her laugh and smile time and time again, as if he'd tapped into her central nervous system and any stimulus, anything at all, resulted in an agreeable mating response. Witnessing this, I wasn't sure whether to applaud his efforts or plunge a sword through his gut in a fit of jealousy.

Of course, I did neither.

I did what the rest of the guys crippled by social paralysis were doing: I drank the skunky beer and repeatedly checked my watch to make it look like I was waiting for someone. After an hour of that pathetic charade, I gave up and did my best to move to the music that was playing at a thousand decibels above what would be deemed a noise violation. I was dancing. I think. Though dancing is supposed to be freeing and human. What I was doing was a series of highly self-regulated movements to ensure that my limbs were in sync and not in danger of harming anyone.

It was neither human nor freeing.

Then this happened: Diana, a fancy diamond in the human form, and entirely out of my perceived league, walked over to me and said, "It looks like my friend and your friend are going to be chatting for a while, so I thought I'd introduce myself. I'm Diana."

Poor Diana was left to chat with me, the worst consolation prize ever, while her girlfriend batted eyelashes and flashed her big teeth and pink gums at Russell. I offered to get Diana a beer, and she told me it wasn't beer they were serving — it was horse piss. She said they had a Clydesdale with a heavy bladder out back and were using him to fill the kegs. That perhaps they should call the beer Draft Horse. She laughed at her own joke while I swirled around what was left in my red plastic cup. I downed it, right then and there, and wholly agreed with her remark. She told me I was brave, and I candidly disagreed with her. I asked Diana what she was taking. She said journalism, and her tone suggested I might think that was unoriginal.

"If you write, you must love to read," I said.

"I do."

"What have you read lately?"

She cracked a smile. One of those half ones where one corner of the mouth turns up, but the other corner isn't yet convinced.

What came out of that horribly awkward conversation-starter was that we had all but shared the same bookcase growing up. I dropped reference after reference of all the greats, and she ate it up ferociously. She asked me what I thought of one book after another, and my responses seemed to dazzle her. She would say words like, "yes," and "absolutely," and "I can't believe you're saying this! I just can't!"

Soon she was batting eyelashes and flashing her teeth and gums at me. She was touching her face and neck and tucking perfect ribbons of hair behind her perfect ears, exposing the definition of her perfect cheekbones. After books, we got onto the subject of the news, and it was very clear that we were two news junkies in a pod. Playfully sparring over who was the best anchor, and why. She said Sterling MacKinnon, which floored me. I jutted out my jaw, tilted my head like a dog hearing its own name, and gave her the best Sterling MacKinnon impression I had in me. The whole thing sounded more like a drunken Sean Connery than the world-renowned news anchor, but she was more than entertained with my effort.

"Do it again!" she said, gasping for air. "One more time, please!"

"Good evening, I'm Sterling MacKinnon … and I just murdered yet another stylist for improperly combing my gorgeous, gorgeous hair." Diana laughed so hard, her nostrils flared and pulsated. The two of us rehashed the worst tragedies of the last decade: natural disasters, conflicts, and elections, and debated which network had covered it best.

Who with the most integrity.

Who with the best spin.

Who with the worst.

Who with the greatest agenda.

This day would go on to be the greatest of my all-too short life.

Some guy at the party yelled last call, and Russell took Diana's friend back to our dorm room. Diana suggested that we go back to hers. She said she made the best French press coffee.

No coffee was had.

Lying there afterward, she asked if that had been my first time, and I confirmed her shrewd hypothesis.

"Honestly, don't worry about it," she said.

"Should I be worried?"

"No, I mean, don't worry about it ... if you were worrying about it. What I'm saying is there's nothing to worry about," she said.

"That's good to hear."

From there, she informed me that I was, in fact, pretty damn interesting and that I should carry myself as if I believed it wholeheartedly.

"Trust me on this; your love for books is your fishing rod and bait."

"Why are you teaching me to fish?"

"Keep asking girls what they've read lately and see what happens," she said. "So far you are one for one. Terrific stats if you ask me."

"I guess you can't argue with math."

"You have a real quality about you," she said and combed my hair with her fingers. "Girls will be bamboozled for one night with a fun, fast-talking guy like Russell, but they'll want a lifetime with a guy like you, Luke. That's a fact. That's your take-away from this evening."

I asked her if that was a backhanded compliment.

She smiled, called me cute, and relaxed into the lighting of a joint. She took an effortless pull of smoke, held it for one one thousand, two one thousand, three one thousand, and then majestically released it into the air, as though having purified any toxins or impurities with her superhuman composition. She rolled to her side and offered the joint up to me.

"I don't. But thanks."

"See, you keep proving my point," she said and took another pull. "Listen to me, Luke, stay the hell out of bars. Never go into a bar again if you're looking to find someone. That's out of bounds for you now. Promise?"

"Promise."

She held out her pinky, and we sealed the deal as pinky fingers do. I didn't ever want that pinky lock to break. Soldered together for life at the pinky would have been fine with me.

• • •

In the morning, after pulling on my wrinkled clothes and stepping into my untied shoes, I stood in her doorway looking for the right words.

"You want to ask me out again, or to hang out another time, right?" she said, like an oracle or something.

"Yes."

"Luke, you don't want me. You're just about to have the time of your life out there. Enjoy it. But you don't want me."

"I think I really do."

"Trust me. You don't."

And I believed her, because I believed everything that came out of her perfect mouth, even if it wasn't what I wanted to hear. If Diana-of-no-last-name had other plans for me … so be it.

Off I went without putting up a fight.

• • •

After Diana-of-no-last-name, there was something to live for again. No longer was I obsessed with my rear-view mirror, my fixation with Death. Diana had reintroduced me to Life. From that pivotal moment forward, I did my best to take her advice and foster situations where I could meet girls with interests like hers. Like my own. Truth be told, I became relatively good at it:

meeting girls at book clubs, book launches, author readings, and anything book-related.

Good, relative to my pals and their success rate at bars.

Their success was little to none, and any perceived successes were deemed remorseful shortly thereafter. Routinely, their nights ended with late-night pizza or jumbo hot dogs with a heaping side order of greasy excuses. Mine ended with the library shutting down for the night and a desire to keep chatting.

Chatting leads to things. Diana taught me that.

My relationship with Life was booming. The looks from the friends in my circle, and the way they treated me, informed the idea of myself, that imaginary self-portrait we paint, to shape-shift. I felt the growing pains of confidence as it multiplied inside me and within the borders of that stretched canvas. Finally, the image I had of myself was something to be proud of. Something you'd want on the mantle at home for your mom to smile at as she walked past it.

Like I said, I was having the time of my life with Life.

Then I graduated.

At commencement, I stood in my cap and gown, listening to the speaker wax philosophic about widespread religious tolerance and what that world might look like in fifty years. I wondered what Diana-of-no-last name might look like that very minute. What she might be up to and who with. I spoke a silent prayer, a silent thank-you to her, as if she were God and able to hear it. She was the one responsible for my rebirth, after all.

• • •

A few short years and a gemology degree later, I moved back home just in time to remember how much I hated it and set up a jewellery boutique in one of my father's commercial buildings. Like a model entrepreneur, I took out some debt, set up the shop with product and began selling high-end watches and diamonds to young men and elderly women looking to spread some inheritance money around before they kicked off. Despite my sincere guidance, this is what always happened: the old women would cheap out and the young men would spend beyond their means. Acts of chest-pounding, all with the help of some prehistoric, compressed carbon that when faceted and polished not only reflected light but also your rung on the social ladder.

Welcome to Oakville.

Home to old wealth, new wealth, and damn near there. Home to private schools with higher yearly tuition than most universities and littered with giant luxury SUVs hauling around petulant children who kick and throw tantrums because they understand the law too well for their own development. High-end shops lining quaint downtown streets and multi-million-dollar homes lining the thickest cut of rough alongside private golf courses that used to be farmers' fields.

Barely real. A mirage.

And it was somewhere in that mirage that I stumbled upon Alice Beck.

Of all my gross indiscretions, this one tops the list: I disobeyed Diana-of-no-last-name's specific orders and met a girl in a bar. She was shorter than me by a foot or so, and the perfume wafting from her hair was intoxicating. Plumeria, as I recall. Upon first glace, I knew that she wasn't for me. This was a girl who liked guys like Russell. I could just tell. People like her were extras in my world — there to populate venues and to add a certain production value to life. People whom I would notice but were somehow instructed not to take any notice of me. And that was fine. This woman at the bar, she was two things: unequivocally an extra, and an obstacle in my path to getting a drink. My arm waved in the air above her scented hair, doing my best to flag down the bartender, but the motion looked more like I was poorly hailing a cab. Snapping fingers turned into something like open-palm window washing, then back to snapping, then devolving into outright pointing.

The bartender looked at me and shook his head, complete with the eyebrow flinch as if to suggest I was mentally ill or something.

"Sorry, are you trying to order a drink, or are you telling the bartender to steal second base?" she said and flashed a teasing smile. "That, or you're conducting an opera."

"It's a tragedy," I said. "The hero dies at the end due to thirst." She smiled again. The whole thing was strange. The extra had not only acknowledged my presence but had now engaged in conversation. Something was wrong. Like I said, typically, I'm invisible to anyone who would be attracted to Russell. It just worked that way. I was confortable in that universe.

She smiled and cupped her hands around her mouth like a coach yelling words of encouragement at a labouring marathoner. "Hey, make it two, please! I need one more!" The bartender didn't even look up; he just nodded. "There," she said. "You're getting a whisky sour."

"Thank you. Listen, the whole round is on me."

"You don't have to do that."

"You seem to have his ear. Why not add a few shots to the mix as well? My treat," I said, and her eyes locked onto mine with something of a death grip.

"Aren't you a fun one," she said and poked me centre mass, right between the ribs charged with the task of protecting my heart. With that initial touch and those five deadly words, she poisoned the well. A dangerous thought was introduced to my brain that I could be the fun one at the bar, just like Russell was, and I ran with it. I abandoned the teachings of Diana, and became someone else for the rest of that night. I took that self-portrait of myself and whitewashed it right then and there. Drinks and shots became a cycle worth repeating, fuelling my growing confidence with each round. She dragged me across the dance floor by the hand and after pinballing off a few dozen people, she introduced me to her friends.

"Isn't he fun and cute!" she shouted over the music. They all smiled and raised their glasses to toast her, like she had accomplished something of great meaning and importance. More poison for the well: I was now being described as both cute and fun — the verbs played hard and loud into my new persona. What would Russell do next? I dragged her by the hand back to the dance floor and we cut loose to a Bon Jovi track, screaming the chorus, the only part anyone ever knows.

We danced.

We laughed.

We kissed.

"I don't even know your name," she said. "I don't kiss random boys on dance floors."

"Luke."

"Alice."

"Stevenson."

"Beck."

"Nice to meet you," I said, and we kissed again.

I had become him. I was Russell, and imagined him leaning up against the oak and brass of the bar, tipping his hat to me with pride and admiration.

• • •

This was New Luke. New Luke went out three to four nights a week with Alice Beck. New Luke partied hard, overspent, and stayed out late. New Luke ate at fancy restaurants with well-educated, well-groomed couples that Alice introduced him to. But most importantly, New Luke loved when Alice Beck would say that he was the most fun guy she had ever dated. Wild. Crazy. More verbs to describe this iteration of me that Old Luke would cross his arms and shake his head at in disbelief. It didn't matter much what Old Luke thought. Because New Luke was, in a word, popular.

This popularity, it infected my body and released a never-ending supply of endorphins to surf through my vasculature. This high, it was the best I had felt in my entire life, and it had to continue, or I thought I might shrivel up and become the worst thing of all: insignificant. Like any quality junkie, New Luke determined that the best course of action was to ensure the stability of the rush by becoming permanently attached to my dealer — Alice Beck. Forever with her — that was New Luke's dream. An infinite supply of late-night partying and rubbing elbows with the popular crowd.

This is what New Luke did in order to foster that dream: he married her.

. . .

Aside from entering that bar in the first place, the biggest mistake I ever made was marrying an entertainment coordinator named Alice. After we settled into marriage, there was nothing entertaining about it, and it was largely my fault. The undeniable fact was this: I had sold Alice a phony bill of goods. The persona of New Luke became as equally impossible to uphold as the expense of the breakneck speed of our lifestyle. After six months with a band on my finger, it was all I could do to show up, smile, hug, shake hands, and order those rounds of drinks and trays of shots, as advertised during the courtship. The jewellery store had picked up significantly and was taking the lion's share of time and energy to make ends meet. Old Luke was dying to lie on a couch on a Friday night and watch a movie or read a book. But the opportunity to do that was a ghost. That inability to decompress, that full social dance card, that ongoing maintenance of my phony persona, grew into a poisonous resentment of New Luke.

Old Luke murdered him.

All that was left after that was little old me. The real me.

And that version of me Alice hated.

Shortly after Alice met the real me, her demeanour, even when intimate, was litigious, and she wore and wore on my confidence to the point where the bone becomes visible and you understand how injured you truly are. Like a dog habitually licking a wound, I licked at my relationship sores for years.

I could taste the infection.

I understood that the prognosis required amputation, but I stayed put in that marriage for five years.

Half a decade.

My father once told me that when your attitude changes, everything changes. But the way I saw it, that particular glass of decade was half-empty. Late one night, over a few too many pints, I said to him, "Alice Beck lied to me, Dad."

"How's that?" he said.

"She not from Milton at all. She's from Hell." He laughed, and that was fine, but it was me who had been the liar. Me, the Oscar-worthy performer who would see no applause, no golden statue, or full spread in the entertainment section. And it was the guilt over what I had done, the deception, that kept me heavily belted and tightly fastened in my marital seat to take the emotional beating she gave me. It was something deserved after the routine I had given her. For the betrayal of my true self.

Alice forged ahead with her own life. She became obsessed with her level of fitness and started working out at the gym several times a week. She hired a hulking personal trainer who beat her up in the early mornings, and she joined a running club that pounded the pavement on nights when we didn't have social engagements. Invariably, she would spill into the house at around ten-thirty at night, unlace, and head directly upstairs for a long shower. To be honest, it was nice to see her sink her teeth into something that was pure. Something that was good for the body, mind, and spirit. Something unlike the rest of her world.

Tammy Yau, one of her running mates, came into the store looking for a tennis bracelet one afternoon, and I made a comment about how late their evening runs went. I said something about how they should be sponsored by 3M, simply for a discount on the reflective tape.

"Luke, what are you talking about?" she said. "Our runs finish at eight." And with a big smile she slapped me on the shoulder like I had made a juvenile error in telling time.

"You must get together for a drink afterward."

"God, no. We all head home."

While I marinated in this fascinating bit of information, Tammy took her sweet time modelling every tennis bracelet I had in the store. One made her wrist look tiny. Another made it appear swollen. One reminded her of her Aunt June. Another had a terrible vibe to it — riddled with bad energy.

"You should get rid of this piece," she said. "All blood diamonds on this one," and offered it back to me as if it were a dead cat she was holding by the tail. I assured her that my diamonds were all conflict-free, but she just shook her head with a furrowed brow. "Impossible," she said. "Those diamonds are dripping."

Eventually she found the one that best spoke to her, and I rang it up, laid it in a velvet box, and tied a bow around it. She left and the bell jingled on the door.

If the running group wrapped things up at eight o'clock, it seemed that jogging might not be all that Alice was sinking her teeth into. Who was this person? Who was shaking my hand at all of these social events and dinner parties with a little extra might in their grip, given the circumstances? Given their silent one-upmanship of me. The only soul I trusted enough with this information was my childhood best friend, Geoff Black. He said, "What do you care, Luke? You can't stand her. This should be good news, no?" And that response startled me both in its candour and lack of empathy. Was she entitled to this imagined act of infidelity? Perhaps this was the second phase of my punishment for pulling the wool over her eyes with the persona of New Luke. If anything,

I simply wanted to put a face to my theory. To sleuth out the truth and feel the comfort of a win in my column. Something to justify moving on. But without proof, my hypothesis was nothing more than a best guess. Try as I might to catch her in the act, she smelled my suspicions. Probing questions were diverted like a jetliner approaching a thunderhead. Alice was far too clever to be caught, certainly not by the likes of me.

Over the years, an embittered Alice managed to turn my confidence, that imaginary self-portrait, into the worst sight of all. A wash of red with deep cuts. Sections of shredded canvas hanging by threads on the crooked, splintered frame.

Nothing recognizable.

No head.

No neck.

No shoulders.

Just something to be collected and discarded, like all those bodies on the news.

And that's how my self-portrait remained until the accident.

2

In the case of my death, it was my birthday. I was racing from work to attend yet another horribly pretentious dinner party with the Greenes. Don and Nancy Greene were our neighbours to the west, but we didn't operate as normal neighbours might. Or should, for that matter. We didn't borrow sugar or lawn chairs or propane tanks. We didn't cook extra food or bake extra cranberry-orange-cinnamon muffins to pass over the fence in goodwill.

We operated differently.

We operated inefficiently as one another's social high-watermark. If the Greenes purchased a new car, Alice demanded we follow suit. Typically something German, with the exception that it must be one or two models higher or with an added feature or luxury package. If the Greenes renovated their kitchen, Alice dug her hand deep into our cookie jar of available credit and updated ours as well, with superior stainless steel appliances and thicker, imported granite.

Granite flown over from some tiny Italian island.

The point is I was working a full-time job for nothing more than the financial means necessary to keep up with the Greenes, playing angel investor in a sickening game of social tennis whereby the wooden trellis separating our two properties might have well been constructed with black nylon netting and a solid white plastic strip. The manicured lawns on both sides of the fence only fully supported this metaphor.

Alice had long accepted the fact that she had married the wrong Luke, but that didn't stop her from winding me up and demanding I play a supporting role in her social opus.

Eventually, I became toxic due to unsafe and prolonged levels of manipulation and verbal abuse. Recurring daydreams became the norm whereby customers were forced to enter my jewellery store in HAZMAT suits just to do business with me, eager to purchase my timepieces and high-quality diamonds, but terrified that they might be exposed to my resentment radiation and fall victim themselves. Double over, vomit blood, and twitch while begging for a quicker death. I imagined the repercussions of my own death, the environmental disaster of my funeral where the government would be forced to bury my poisoned body hundreds of feet under the earth, inside a thick rubber bladder, so that my resentment wouldn't seep into and contaminate the groundwater. In one daydream, they simply threw me in alongside used plutonium rods to ensure safekeeping.

Back to the Greenes.

One year, Nancy Greene bought a Christmas tree that brushed the top of their soaring fifteen-foot living-room ceiling. Truthfully, it was the most spectacular Christmas tree I had ever laid eyes on. Perfectly trimmed and shaped, as if it were made from some high-end polymer. But nothing in their house was fake except Nancy's breasts.

And nose. I had always suspected her chin, although that wasn't verified until after my death. Nancy looked like the well-dressed, well-accessorized mannequin at Holt Renfrew had kicked out the storefront glass and marched down Bloor Street programmed to seek and destroy a gentle, hard-working man who might be willing to play the sport of social tennis. That man turned out to be Don Greene.

Back to the Christmas tree.

It was a storybook tree that Nancy had, of course, found herself. The fantastical tale she told of locating said tree lacked only the inclusion of unicorns and Sherpa leprechauns who spoke Old English … leading Nancy to her magnificent conifer. Nancy passionately explained that the majority of the ornaments were purchased from Swarovski, a high-end crystal retailer, and that she had hired a Christmas Tree Consultant to help her decorate the towering pine behemoth that now occupied the lion's share of their living room.

"It was so darn difficult to track her down, she's so in demand these days," said Nancy. "But didn't she work the lights and ornaments like a magician? Am I right, or am I right. Right? Exactly."

Alice and I stood in amazement.

Here's the difference in our perspective: The amazement Alice was experiencing was due to increased, self-inflicted social pressure given the state of our current Christmas tree, dressed with family heirlooms and other antique ornaments handmade from blown glass. Our humble tree sported painted eggshells, God's Eyes knit from wool, poorly dyed plastic icicles, and snowflakes made from paper cutouts. Each ornament was chock full of sentimental value and incapable of a price tag. However, when compared to Nancy's Christmas Tree 2.0, ours was truly an epic failure.

That was Alice's perspective.

My amazement centred around the fact that there were Christmas Tree Consultants who charged people the equivalent of a mortgage payment. I felt burning in my throat. An antisocial comment was in the process of breaking out, and I did my best to swallow it, but it was coming up hot like a burp of acid reflux. A full sweat was broken into during my last-ditch efforts to contain it, but the comment had firmly taken root in my larynx, and this is what I blurted: "Nancy, why the hell did you spend all this money decorating something that's in the process of dying?"

Nancy straightened up, at a loss for words.

Alice turned away.

And in walked Don Greene, as if on cue. He sauntered into the living room holding two fish-bowl-sized brandy snifters, and this is what he said: "Isn't that all we are, good buddy? Two decorated Christmas Trees in the process of dying?"

Point — Don.

Fifteen love.

That level of candour for our respective situations was both admirable and entirely disgusting. In passing me my brandy, his triceps muscle revealed itself from underneath his form-fitting cashmere sweater. Athletic, yes, and he was always impeccably dressed. Don looked like a well-groomed, real-life Ken doll, except for his battle with psoriasis.

With respect to Don's wardrobe, Alice would always say, "Don, you look so sharp!"

Don would smile and say, "Oh, these old rags?" and then wink. The wink was there to denote his full understanding that the garments were the furthest from rags, and to thank her for noticing. This is also true: Don Greene finished seven out of ten sentences with a wink.

His stab at boyish teasing.

His stab at charm.

So often I wanted to thumb out that winking eye so it could no longer continue offending. Like hacking off the hands of a thief or something. Clothing aside, Don, like me, was nothing more than a financier in a game of social chess, and I didn't want to be on the board at all. Was he the prick, the one meeting Alice in some godforsaken rent-by-the-hour motel after running club? The answer was always no in my mind. They found too much common ground chitchatting about fine wines and the new arrivals at Pottery Barn to be entangled in a raging affair.

Back to the Christmas tree.

Don looked up at their enormously gaudy tree and sighed, as if entirely impressed with the bedazzled blue spruce. Like a pharaoh looking upon a pyramid post-construction.

"Isn't it something, Luke?" he said. "Isn't it like Christmas was born here?"

I recall wanting to splinter his larynx into his vocal chords so that no more offensive upper-middle-class utterings would be possible. Of course, I'd never do that. Candidly, part of me admired Don for having the ability to turn off his brain and submit to Nancy's dictatorship, as if he was a Darwinian mutation of modern man. It just seemed so much easier.

This was my reply: "It certainly does seem that Christmas was born here, Don." And then we clinked fishbowls and drank. Rudely, I took down the extra-old brandy in a single gulp.

"Hey, go easy on the top-shelf booze," he said. I refused to acknowledge the comment. There was Nancy, in front of me, deep in the process of going over each Swarovski ornament, one by one, with Alice. Each new crystal drove a glistening spike into my wife's paper-thin confidence. The burning question in my mind revolved around how Alice was going to respond to Nancy's powerful cross-court winner of a Christmas tree.

Here's how she did it: Lacking fifteen-foot ceilings of our own, Alice did the only thing she could to compete with Nancy Greene that particular Christmas. Days later, she purchased a second eight-foot tree, because two times eight made sixteen feet, and that was exactly one more foot of Christmas tree than Nancy had. We now had one tree for the living room, and one for the family room. Both were dressed in prohibitively expensive ornaments. Many of them, the Swarovski leftovers that Nancy had passed over in the store, were marked down as part of a clearance sale. Down came the family heirlooms from our original tree — wrapped, boxed, and taped up heavily, never to release the ghosts of Embarrassing Ornaments of Christmas past.

• • •

During this miserable period, I had rekindled my relationship with Death, and we became good pals again. This go-around he wasn't nearly as feared, sitting back there behind my driver's seat in all of this ugliness. We spoke often, which consisted of me attempting to make deals with him. Like clockwork, after a massive blow-up with Alice, I would adjust the rearview mirror, look him in the eye sockets, and make an offer for him to take me now.

"What's it going to take, Death?" I would say.

Death would scratch the heavily rotted section of his face with the legs of his tarantula hand and then shake his head.

His refusal to take me was horrible news. It meant the continuation of my relationship with Alice and the Greenes, an unaffordable tango, doable only because of the precarious wonder of credit.

All the while, Alice continued to reinvent her own coping mechanisms to deal with our terrible marriage. Alice's identity and entire self-worth became what she wore, what she drove, what she lived in, what she drank, what she ate, and with whom and how often. Because of all that, she had established quite a name for herself in our neighbourhood as an impeccable host. Five-course meals. Artisan breads. Desserts made in small boutique shops that everyone remembered the names of except me. Polished silver. Crystal glasses and decanters. Pressed linen tablecloths. Silk napkins. It was five-star every time company was seated, and when (on occasion) we happened to be the guests, she always brought the finest wine.

"It's from Napa," she would say. "It's out of this world. You are going to just die."

Three out of seven days of the week warranted some form of dinner or cocktail gathering, and the subject of conversations was always this: other people's kids.

What they were up to.

Their teachers.

Their schools.

The cost of their schools.

And the myriad verbs that defined their infinite cuteness. Every story ended with, "They just grow up so fast," and everyone listening would nod and say, "It's so true, isn't it?"

Then everyone would drink, as if to reminisce.

But I wouldn't agree.

I did, however, participate in the group drink portion of the conversation. A hefty pull on my Scotch, as if happiness were somewhere near the bottom of the glass, and I were drowning in an attempt to get there.

For Alice, talking about other people's kids provided some form of anesthetic due to the fact we had none to speak of ourselves. It was an emerging social requirement to add to the checklist. Despite the fact that she wholly detested and held an unhealthy amount of resentment toward me, she did attempt to get pregnant from time to time. Which, of course, wreaked havoc on my theory of infidelity. Why further anchor yourself to someone you loathe except to keep up appearances? Perhaps this guy on the side was supposed to set up camp and live exclusively in the shadows of her life, existing only between the hours of eight and ten, a few days a week. Something to be used, cleaned, and put away until next time, like a rowing machine. Regardless, I had been called upon to play husband and perform the simplest of nature's tasks. However, no luck. The strip was always one single line and not two.

This seemed to be my fault.

No, we didn't bother asking science to definitively make a ruling on the matter. It was simply easier if it was my fault, and I would say nothing when she blamed it on the cut of my underwear, or my penchant for wearing that underwear to bed, or the shape of the seat on my cycling machine in the basement, or that I really didn't want to have kids, which was negatively affecting the physical integrity of sperm.

"I bet that's it," she would say to me. "Isn't it? Your negative thinking and not wanting children is making your sperm retarded.

They've lost their natural GPS and can't find the fucking egg! I need this, Luke. It's the least you can give me."

What was I left to do but stand and stare?

Vacantly.

Void of any intelligent or witty comeback, as if an alien had crash-landed on my property and was standing in my designer kitchen, cooking poached eggs in a Pottery Barn apron and attempting to communicate with me. And there I stood, frozen in her tractor beam of nonsense.

The truth is this: the thought of having kids with Alice and having intercourse with Alice became equally as terrifying. Both would result in orders being barked in my direction, followed by an error of the grandest scale on my part, and ultimately, wearing the blame for an improper turnout. On several occasions, I thought I would rather die than have a child with Alice. I'm not sure if this particular plea with Death caused it to happen, but here's how my life came to an abrupt end.

Rushing to my forced birthday party with the Greenes caused me to travel a handful of kilometres-per-hour faster than the law deemed appropriate. Rushing, the sin of lost perspective, landed my car smack-dab in the middle of an intersection several seconds early, which allowed for the perfect timing of a complete stranger fumbling with his cellphone to run a red light and hitting me square in the driver's-side door.

An explosion on impact accompanied by the unwilling whine of twisting metal. Steel and glass having breached many sections of me. You'd think after an impact like that the lights go out, but I had several moments of lucid thought.

In those final moments, I imagined Alice drinking the fabulous wine from Napa with the Greenes, checking her Cartier automatic timepiece with 1.77 carats worth of excellently cut VVS1, F-colour diamonds spread out along the bezel, apologizing for my tardiness and lack of manners.

"I can't believe he's doing this," I imagined her saying. "Who is late for their own birthday party? It's so typical. It's so embarrassing."

Sitting there, bleeding out, I flashed back to the week before — my mother hugging me desperately after my weekly visit for tea and a game of gin rummy. She pulled me in tight on the weathered veranda and whispered, "They've got it all wrong, Luke. You're the catch. Not her. That's the truth of the matter. Try to remember that."

She kissed my cheek and rubbed my back, as if I were terminally ill and she was doing her best to heal what remained of me.

At this point, with only moments of life to spare, my frantic mind went to Diana-of-no-last-name, fast-forwarding through the greatest day of my life. I felt a smile adorn my dripping, broken face.

What I had finally recognized was true love.

Not lust.

Not love with asterisks.

Not love in sheep's clothing.

Just love.

I loved her.

I loved Diana-of-no-last-name.

And my canvas, my self-portrait, began to straighten up. The splintered wood frame pulled itself together, became strong and cohesive, and the angles were ninety degrees again. The shredded canvas stitched itself together, and the red wash dripped off, revealing the choppy strokes of a palate knife, and I could almost make out a face.

And that heart or face or whatever looked happy.

And that was it.

I died on my birthday in the process of falling in love.

• • •

The next thing I knew, I was standing in the Post-Death Line, waiting to meet the Bookkeeper.

3

The Post-Death Line is a shock to any recently deceased individual. No matter how in tune with the universe and liberal-thinking you may be, you are entirely unprepared for what comes directly after death. I'll say this: Those who arrive banking on adopted religious promises are utterly rattled to the core.

Shock.

Panic.

Confusion.

Anger.

All of the above, but never none of the above.

The deeply religious tend to falsely identify the Post-Death Line as Hell or purgatory or a similar equivocation of religious punishment. Others begin to frantically review their lives on Earth in an attempt to determine where they went wrong — how they had failed to please God. And the very few, like myself, who hadn't a clue what was in store after death, quickly turn shock into wonderment and soak up the experience completely. My personal thrill surrounded the fact that the lights hadn't simply gone out; that there was more to life than to grow and maintain a living body, only to end up a smorgasbord for bacteria.

Open-minded or closed, agnostic or fundamentalist, no one is prepared for the Post-Death Line. And being unprepared is without fault. As humans, the one thing we are all guilty of is living in the world. You can't pick the continent or country of your parents, nor can you pick their belief system. We become bombarded with right and wrong from an early age. We are hammered into form like a blacksmith shapes wrought iron and, generally, we do our best to fit in with the herd. We become consumed by stories and promises and drink it all in. There is power in words and in numbers. We remove ourselves from what's real and hang on to what sounds good.

The Line gets all of this sorted out rather quickly and efficiently. Here's how it works:

Imagine the impossibly long lines at customs after an international flight or two has landed. Lines chock full of people from varying countries and creeds, all ripe with unique experiences and stories to tell. Imagine each line running parallel to one another and place tens of thousands of people in each row. Now arrange those lines as if they are the steel spokes on a bicycle wheel, attached to a centre core.

Where the spokes meet the core is where the Bookkeeper exists. Many of him, actually.

Copies of him, shoulder to shoulder, hand in hand, like a string of paper dolls. And the Bookkeeper stands there, receiving the recently deceased after they have made their way to the front of the Post-Death Line.

Admittedly, I have no idea what comes after the Line. I just know it's called What's Next. But the babies seemed to know. They would race to get there. Anyone two years of age or younger floated and criss-crossed between the Post-Death Lines like a bicycle courier in traffic. These babies, they just flew to the front of the lines and past the Bookkeeper instantaneously, without any briefing, discussion, or information exchange.

For the rest of us, those old enough to have forgotten about What's Next; for those of us affected by the world and attached to dogmatic and cultural untruths, the adjustment takes much longer, which is the ultimate purpose of the Line. Said differently, the Post-Death Line gives back to us the most important thing we have lost on account of living in the world: perspective.

Each spirit spends the exact same amount of time in line, and I can't tell you how long that is because time is relative. When you first arrive at the back of your line, you face forward, toward another spirit who, in turn, is facing you. Without prompting or coaching, you connect and download the entirety of that spirit's life on Earth.

You live it as they did.

Through their eyes.

As if it were your story, and you were starring in it.

You experience every high and low and in between and, in tandem, the spirit you have connected with lives your life as if it were their own. When the amount of time for information exchange is complete, the Bookkeeper shifts the spokes of the Post-Death Lines, changing them like a Rubik's Cube. This shift moves you to another line, and you, in turn, rotate, facing the opposite direction. Now you stand with your back to the Bookkeeper, but one spot closer to him. After each connection, your RP (Required Perspective) improves by one. For the second experience, I connected and lived the life of an Afghani woman whose pregnant body had been stoned to death. I lived her life as if it were my own and experienced her death, just as she had. I experienced the pounding fear as my own flesh and blood surrounded me, pointed fingers, and cast the first rocks. I felt the ones that broke my ribs. I felt the ones that shattered my arms as I attempted to shield my face. I felt the matte thud and hot sting of the rock that got through and crushed my nose. The warm metallic taste of blood after the rock to the mouth, and then the one that doubled me over after hitting my pregnant belly. I remember falling after that one, and the blurred vision. The loss of hearing. I recall hoping the baby couldn't feel any of it. Then one more direct hit to the face, and then black.

And that was the end of that life.

The lines shifted, and I lived the life of a British man who died at forty-one, fatally knifed at a rock concert for blocking someone's view.

Then I was a Thai woman who slipped in the tub at ninety-four.

Then I was an American man who died of prostate cancer.

Then I battled and lost to cancer again.

Then I lost my life to the common cold, believe it or not.

Then I was bitten by a venomous snake while picking bananas.

Then I crashed a float plane into a mountain.

Then I was struck by a golf ball in the temple.

Then a heart attack.

Then of pneumonia.

Then due to hanging by the neck during autoerotic asphyxiation.

Then of infection.

Then of childbirth.

Many of childbirth.

Of course, press repeat on this process. Facing forward and then backward. Living and dying in all sorts of exciting and horrific ways.

With each shift of the Line, you move closer and closer to the centre core until, thousands of lives later, you arrive at the Bookkeeper and with Required Perspective. Skin colour, culture, religion, and geography provide nothing more than a contextual backdrop to set the stage for the all-too-similar stories surrounding the human condition.

Simply put, the Post-Death Line is where we all learn how exactly similar we are. The Line is where we shed everything we were taught and cleanse our spirits; wipe clean our hard drives, so to speak, through the process of experience. The blinding veil of misinformation wearing away as the spread of enlightenment accelerates with every life lived. The return to Perspective must be gradual so as not to ruin a spirit. Like a scuba diver slowly returning to the surface, the same is true with our spiritual composition. It can be soured if the process of unlearning and relearning is not handled with care.

• • •

By the time I faced the Bookkeeper, I had lived 19,251 lives. He offered to connect with me. I accepted. From the Bookkeeper, I was able to download my original Time Card. Whoever presides over What's Next clearly identifies for how long each spirit is released to Earth. Thus, when our spirits are delivered, they come attached with this information. Think of it like dog tags. The Time Card shows a Spirit Number, Date of Delivery, and Date of Reintegration.

"Date of Reintegration was your understanding of death," said the Bookkeeper. True, but what struck me was that my Date of Reintegration was many years farther along in the earthly calendar. How could that be the case? How had I been robbed of time on my lease?

"I have a question."

"Surrounding the fact that you were taken too early," he said.

"It looks that way, yes."

"You have a very important choice to make, Luke," he said, and explained the situation I was in.

It turned out that due to the car accident, due to the interference of another individual having run that red light and ending my time on Earth, my options consisted of the following: moving on to What's Next or returning to Earth in order to live out the remainder of my designated spirit lease as a ghost, back among the living.

This seemed a fair proposition given that I had been robbed of exactly fifty-five years, eleven months, three days, three hours, six minutes, and forty-six point eight two seconds.

"And not everyone gets this choice?" I said.

"This decision applies only to those whose Time Card was unfairly affected by another being," he said and then uploaded to me all of the conditions that defined "Human Interference."

Famine was added to the List of Human Interference in 1935, since (by that time) there was more than enough food to feed the world many times over, and the means to deliver it promptly. Thus, death due to starvation on account of global hoarding and improper distribution was deemed unfair by whoever presides over What's Next. Death by Infant Disease was the most recent addition, in 1992, since by that time the lack of inoculation was deemed Human Interference. Death by acquiring HIV through sexual intercourse, injection, in utero, or through childbirth had been added several years before that.

"The guy who hit me. What happened to him?" I asked.

"He was forced to What's Next."

And then the Bookkeeper sent me the life story of Gregory Adam Charles, which was as fascinating as any other until he was texting his way through an intersection. Affecting his Time Card was his own fault, but he clearly wasn't supposed to T-bone and dismember me in the process.

"Under what conditions does anyone choose to return as a ghost?" I said, and the Bookkeeper sent me exactly one million examples and their corresponding determining factors. Once analyzed, it seemed most were between the ages of eight and seventy; those who still had close friends and family on Earth and wanted to spend more time alongside them; those who wished to be present for graduations and weddings and births. Others wanted to see how certain earthly stories played out, like who would win the World Series, for example.

Or the World Cup. The Olympics, or an important election.

Who would win a war.

"What do you suggest for me?"

He sent me my life story in the form of a digital document, with the flashing cursor marking my current location in the story. What followed the flashing cursor was an infinite number of blank pages, and I understood.

"Your decision, please," he said.

. . .

I elected to return to Earth. Even with Required Perspective at 100 percent, curiosity is the one thing wherein perspective can fail you. Burning questions need answering, and regardless of how many lives you've lived, curiosity is not something easily overcome. A gut feeling left unconfirmed is sour milk for the soul. The decision to return involved the two largest mysteries in my world: the truth surrounding my notion of Alice's infidelity, and to identify the location and condition of the true love of my life, Diana-of-no-last-name.

"You're certain," said the Bookkeeper.

"I am. Yes."

"Understand that as a ghost you will be unable to perform any action that would change what was meant to be, or the course of history," he said.

"I understand."

"You have been assigned a Mentor Spirit. His name is Robert F. Sutherland. You are to connect with him within twenty-four hours of arriving back on Earth as a spirit," he said, and then I downloaded from the Bookkeeper who he was, and how to contact him. "Your Mentor Spirit is the only spirit you'll be able to see or communicate with at first."

"Then what?"

"Shortly after you meet with Robert and spend some time on Earth, you'll be a Mentor yourself, ready to train a Recently Delivered Spirit (RDS) on global travel and to be there for them, should they wish to connect, for whatever reason. After your return to Earth, you will remain there in your new form for fifty-five years, eleven months, three days, three hours, six minutes, and forty-six point eight two seconds — the remainder of your spirit lease."

The Bookkeeper uploaded to me the Code of Conduct and set of laws surrounding Ghosting and the Mentorship program.

This was called *The Ghosting Handbook*.

I read and accepted everything presented to me and sent him back the document, having initialled all of the pages.

"Do we ever correspond?" I said.

"If you wish, you can formally submit questions or comments," and he sent me that section of the *Handbook* highlighted in hot pink. "Think of it like an upload. I respond as quickly as I can, but understand that I have my hands full with the Post-Death Line. I'm not an all-seeing eye."

After we discussed John F. Kennedy, Area 51, and the Loch Ness Monster, he sent me back to Earth as a Recently Delivered Spirit.

I elected to arrive at the scene of my own funeral.

4

I hovered over my open casket. Not for any dramatic effect or to be spooky; it was simply the best seat in the house. Strange to look down on yourself from this perspective. There lay my body, vacated by the inhabitant and its framework left to break down like that of an abandoned building. Something to be looked at but not touched. Something that can't be restored. That said, the mortician had worked a small miracle with his attempt to bring the abandoned building back to life. Given the extent of my injuries, to have an open casket was both an act of bravery and true artistry. The stitch lines holding my face together were barely visible underneath all of the foundation and bronzer. My corpse seemed to have acquired an unusual overbite, which spoke to the fact that my jawbone had fallen out of place somewhere in transit. Undoubtedly, more adhesive bonding was required at the hinges. That, or my teeth should have been glued together as a failsafe — what was left of them. I can't imagine there being a full set of pearly whites in there given the severity of the impact. That was only confirmed by the fact that my lips had been glued shut. The weight of the unsecured jawbone was pulling the cemented lips into something of a frown or a look of distaste. Should the glue give way, my mouth would surely gape open, exposing all the nubs and sharp angles of broken teeth.

All in all, I looked pretty good for having been put back together. An extreme makeover: monster edition. My eyebrows had been shaped and pencilled in where sections were missing, and the random hairs growing on my earlobes had been removed. Alice had been on my case for years about those guys. Who knew this was what it would take to finally get that checked off the to-do list? My hair was heavily gelled and glistened under the lights of the church, like I was set to play Danny in a high school production of *Grease*. Parted and styled the way Alice preferred it — Second World War pilot style. It was the only part of me that looked heroic.

My hands, which had also been given a thick layer of foundation, were folded neatly over my navel. Upon further inspection, my left hand seemed to be resting at an impossible angle, leading me to believe that it wasn't attached to anything. The unnatural, puffy-looking sleeve of the suit they had managed to contort me into gave more proof that the entire left arm was missing. They had stuffed it with cotton batting or fiberfill in the spirit of smoke and mirrors. And as much as I appreciated the efforts of the mortician, I couldn't help but think that Alice had demanded the open casket. A final farewell to the Luke she married and the Luke she got. An art installation suggesting that things might not be as they seem. That one should peel back a few layers down before buying the advertising.

The place was crammed, filled with colourful floral arrangements and people dressed in black. Some people I hadn't seen or spoken to in years. People I never imagined would attend something like this.

Not for me.

Reverend Rundle stood at the pulpit.

"Luke James Stevenson," he said. "The man responsible for so many diamond rings and happy moments in this very room. It's hard to associate him with anything as tragic as today. You know,

I remember as if it was yesterday … when Luke stood up here for his Confirmation."

Confirmation. Yes, who could forget that? Bob Graham was in my Confirmation class, and I downright hated Bob. In addition to Sunday sermons, Bob could also be found during the weekdays in my class at school, which left Saturday as the only true day of rest. Except that Bob lived just down the street from me in a small red-brick bungalow.

Number forty-three. The one with two chimneys, one mom, and six boys.

Bob was gender agnostic when it came to terrorizing and belittling, tearing down and intimidating. Even in the purported safety of the classroom, he would play sniper and fire a dozen or more spitballs a day at those he had chosen to torture. He was Billy the Kid with a wide-band broccoli elastic, lined paper, and thick saliva. If your name happened to rank high on the hate list, Bob would bypass the hair entirely and snipe you with a head shot. The spit bullet would stick to your cheek for a second and then slowly begin to snail down the face. Head-shot victims would scream and scratch wildly to remove the spitball, as if Bob's saliva had penetrated the cheek and was in the process of infecting. The teacher would whip around and say, "What's wrong? What is it? What happened!"

But no one tattled on Bob the Bully.

Yet Sunday after Sunday, there he was, sitting in the church pew beside the five aspiring bullies-in-training who all shared a last name. The fox in the henhouse.

And the fox would sing and pray and say amen when prompted. He would carry on as if equal to the rest of us in God's eyes. Then again, why wouldn't he? We were told time and time again that God loved us all the same. The reverend would say these words, and I would grit my teeth. My nostrils would flare, and I would force a lungful of breath out of them in frustration. Based on his acts outside of the four sacred walls, how could someone of his moral fabric possibly make it to Heaven? For saying out loud that Jesus was his Lord? Sure, I heard him say it, but in the eighth grade, even that seemed too simple for me; it was nothing but a set of loopholes through which misbehaviour was washed clean with catchphrases and exemplary attendance. And that was exactly what I said to Reverend Rundle during my pre-Confirmation meeting. The comment was sloughed off, and I was instructed to have faith in the process. Then I said, "Bob Graham belongs in Hell."

"That kind of judgmental talk is out of line in God's house," he said. It was at this precise moment that I felt the need to distance myself from faith. From religion. From Reverend Rundle.

"If Bob Graham is going to Heaven," I said. "Then I don't want to be there."

I watched him wriggle in his seat, stroking his greying beard, digging deep within the folds of his sanctified brain for an enlightened ping to my pong. The reverend was typically so prepared with something well-rehearsed, as if divinity school had consisted of memorizing one-liners in response to questions of faith, complete with the condescending delivery and professorial smirk. He picked his ear, sat back, crossed his fat arms, and rolled the waxy green finding between his ring finger and thumb. Eventually it dried, cracked, turned to dust, and disappeared.

He leaned forward, and this was his righteous answer: "Luke, Heaven is a big place. I'm sure you won't bump into Bob up there when the time comes."

And that was that.

A holy union of idiocy and defeat, and I was playing ringbearer for the main event. To me, the only thing Confirmation confirmed was that Reverend Rundle had no idea what he was talking about, and that with religion, if you don't know the answer to a challenging question, you simply make one up — whether responding to a question of faith, biblical interpretation, or the approximate square footage of Heaven.

After a forced apology for sentencing Bob Graham to Hell, I went through with the Confirmation to please my mother.

At thirteen, that's just what you do.

Try to please Mom.

Back to my funeral.

Instinctively, I managed to move from hovering over my open casket to moving directly above Reverend Rundle. He patted his forehead with a handkerchief embroidered with the cross.

"It was those many years ago, as a young man, when Luke was confirmed and voiced that he had accepted Jesus into his heart as his Lord and Saviour. And before that, upon his baptism, in this very church, in the name of Jesus Christ, Luke's spirit was transformed to that of God's Children. In Roman's 6:23, Paul tells us 'the wage is death.' In Jesus there is life. Luke chose Life. He chose an eternity in Heaven, where he is now at peace, sitting at the right hand of the Lord."

Some people said, "Amen."

"At times like this, in times of grief, we tend to question our faith, but God has a plan. He has a great plan for Luke, even in death. Mark my words, God called Luke for a higher purpose. In death there is life. Look around. God brought us all here today. Perhaps some of you may find life today at this tragic time."

Some people spoke out from the congregation.

"Yes," they said.

"Amen," they said.

Someone rattled a tambourine.

It was Mabel Albright, my neighbour when I was growing up. She brought it along to every service and funeral. She believed the sound of it punctuated the important messages, as if to advise that non-believers pay attention.

"So I suggest that in this time of sadness," he said, "we reflect on our relationship with Luke, *and* with God," he said, as if he was a salesman tugging on the fear-strings of not having health or home insurance. "Because God is real, and death is real, and God is there for us in life and in death."

Mabel rattled her tambourine.

Alice sobbed and asked for handfuls of Kleenex from my mother, who emptied her stash to help capture the ocular and nasal drippings of my former Earth-mate. She sure made a lot of noise given that only three of those tears were sincere.

I know this because I read her thought projections. As it turned out, I could read everyone's thoughts. In the *Handbook*, I had read that this was hardwired into every ghost: the ability to connect with the thoughts and visions, daydreams, fantasies, and nightmares of the living. They appear quite vividly.

The whole thing is quite impressive.

Thus, connecting with Alice informed me, in the highest of definition, that she felt she should increase her crying and wailing to cover up the fact she was having an impassioned affair with my childhood best friend, Geoff Black.

And just like that, the first of the two burning mysteries was answered.

Rage filled my new form presenting itself as a shift in my vibrational pattern. I felt radiant, as if glowing white hot. Like I might come apart in a million scorching molecules that would rain down on the congregation, curl hair, and burn scalps. Perspective flooded in shortly thereafter and did its best to smother the rage. Who was I to be enraged? The truth was, I had been an adulterer many times over living people's lives in the Post-Death Line. What kind of hypocrite was I to feel this way?

I moved to hover over the second offender.

There sat Geoff Black.

Three rows back on the far aisle seat.

Geoff was wearing blue Adidas gym socks with his black dress pants and dress shoes. He was very self-conscious about this. He wondered if anyone would notice these athletic socks, since he was now seated, and his dress pants had crept slightly up his leg. He wondered if the pants had pulled up high enough to reveal the universally recognized white logo. *Is there a band of hairy skin showing between the top of the socks and the bottom of my pants?* He thought he shouldn't have rushed to get dressed and concluded that the extra few minutes to find proper matching dress socks would be paying dividends at present. Above all, he feared that everyone would think Alice's affected tears were just that, phony as a three-dollar bill. Geoff's tears, as it turned out, were entirely genuine, albeit mostly guilt-driven, attached to apologies in my direction for being such a terrible friend and doing such a terrible thing.

I replayed the best of our long history together and vibrated with anger at points where we had recently spent time together. Again, I had lived a life like this one in the Line. I had done this exact thing with a best friend's wife. Perspective came pumping in hard now as I replayed those lives and felt the process of calming down.

Anger slowed to annoyance.

Annoyance to empathy.

I wanted to do something to put his grief to rest. To let him know that I forgave him. Fully. That I knew exactly how torn up his guts felt. But all I could do was hover and stream his thoughts. He called himself a pile of bad names over what he had done. He thought about going to a biker bar and picking a fight with someone far bigger just to seek sufficient punishment for his crime. Large fists beat his face to a pulp, and he spat bloodied teeth from his mouth but smiled widely the entire time, thanking the large biker. Geoff even paid the man's tab. He picked his bloody Chiclets off the filthy bar floor and requested a glass of milk to put them in so the roots and nerves would have a chance to live. This was so that his dentist might hammer them back in to place with a mallet and no anesthetic. Geoff thought he'd never use anesthetic again.

Even for heart surgery or any kind of surgery, for that matter. No more pain relief. Not for poor Geoff.

He didn't deserve it.

His eyes crept to their corners, and he looked over to Alice who (in turn) looked over her shoulder at him. The two adulterers pulled forward their most recent sexual encounter with one another. Geoff buried his head in his hands and cried for thinking about something like that at my funeral. Eventually, I needed a break from his misery and moved on to someone else.

Beside Geoff sat Annabelle, his unsuspecting wife, who was also quite surprised so many people had attended. She thought the turn-out was due to Alice's popularity and had nothing to do with me. She thought if people hadn't shown up, Alice would have noticed and would have talked behind their backs. That she would have pitted other women against them in a fit of retaliation. Annabelle spent most of the ceremony terrified that the strange sensation at the tip of her nose could very well be an exposed and hardened booger peeking out for the world to see. *How mortifying*, she thought. She rubbed her nose with her hand and scratched the tip with her index finger every thirty seconds or so.

Five rows back, Suzanne Leroux wondered how she might kill her husband, a chronic snorer, who refused to see a doctor about it. She thought that sleep deprivation due to snoring was a form of both torture and spousal abuse and wondered if she could plead insanity. She thought about smothering him with a pillow. Getting on top of him and pinning the pillow to the mattress with her knees. She thought about snipping her husband's fingers off with garden shears, should he attempt to claw the pillow away. *Snip, snip, snip*, she thought, and the fingers fell on the white pillowcase, making little red circles start the process of expanding into one another. *How am I going to get all that red out?* Then she wondered why she hadn't opened the strawberry jam she purchased at the farmers' market for her toast that morning.

My mother was torn to pieces over the fact that she hadn't sent my birthday card earlier in the month, so I could have taken in what she wrote before the accident, but she thought about what she wrote, and because of that, I was able to read it. She wondered why Alice was crying so much and thought she didn't believe a lick of it. She wondered what the little bitch was covering up and used those words exactly. She wondered if the little bitch had hired someone to smash into me and kill me for the insurance money. She wondered if people would enjoy the sandwiches she had made, and if the mayonnaise might give them all food poisoning. She wondered if she would care if everyone got food poisoning, because hardly anyone there was close to me, besides Geoff Black. She was glad he was there. She would have to make a point of finding him after the service for a big hug. Mom looked over and saw how hard he was crying. *Friends for life, those two*, she thought, and welled up again. She wondered how her heart could possibly heal and under what conditions healing could occur after having to bury her son. She told God to go to Hell. She said to Him, *If this is your plan … consider me out of the game.* She wondered why she had bothered wearing Spanx to my funeral. She thought, *What the hell do I care what these people think about my dimply ass and tummy?*

My father didn't physically cry, but he sobbed internally. A series of swallowing and repeatedly clearing his throat was required to keep his tears trapped beneath the surface. A good man with a good heart who sadly subscribed to definitions of "manliness" passed down many generations.

Light years off the mark.

I'd love to be there when he stands in the Post-Death Line and gains perspective, as per the truth on the subject of gender. He wondered if he had been a good father or not. He thought, *I could have been easier on him*, but he wasn't sure how to get my nose out of the fantasy world of books and into the real world. He thought he should have read the books I begged him to read when I was a teen, so we could've had something to talk about. He thought he would take Mom on a vacation and try to make her laugh more. He thought the brakes needed fixing on his Chevy Impala and shouldn't squeak like they did on the way to the church. Certainly not on a car that age.

My sister, Brooke, cried real tears.

All of them.

She wished we had spent more time together and felt frustrated that, after I had met and married Alice, she saw and heard less of me. Which was true. Tear production increased when Brooke wished she had said something about it, which might have inspired one or both of us to try harder to connect more often. Of anyone in the room, Brooke felt the deepest sense of loss. She thought her heart would never heal. She wondered why so many flakes had shown up to the funeral and then assumed they were here for Alice and not for me at all. She held the hand of her husband, Taitt Champion, a stockbroker for a local money management firm called Reliance Asset Management. She worried Taitt was pulling away from her. *He isn't the same,* she thought. *Something is wrong,* she thought, and decided to bring up her concerns on the drive home from the funeral.

It was true, and she was very right — something was wrong with Taitt. He was not in good shape at all. As the stock market continued to crash outside the confines of the church, Taitt sat quietly at my funeral with charts, numbers, and red arrows flying through his mind. A flood of images attached to sound bites of client voicemails played in a loop in his head, some livid, some terrified, many weeping. Some trading off between weeping and yelling, since their life savings had been wiped away by Taitt's efforts. I connected with Taitt for quite a while during the service. As his forthcoming nervous breakdown rapidly approached, Taitt constructed an animated children's story in his mind involving a Sea Snake named Snee.

You see, the Land Snakes, who were poor swimmers, needed a Sea Snake to navigate them to Retirement Island. So Snee volunteered to lead the journey to Retirement Island, since he was an excellent swimmer. All of the Land Snakes who had signed up to make the trip were in agreement — Snee would be the leader. All was going quite well. He was doing a fine job, but an unexpected storm arose that took Snee and the Land Snakes by surprise. The Land Snakes asked Snee to turn back, but Snee was sure that he could navigate them through the storm to safety. "Keep going!" screamed Snee. "We can't deviate now!"

Sadly, all the Land Snakes drowned.

Snee, now overcome with guilt, fell limply to the dark depths at the bottom of the sea. He dug deep into the mud of the ocean floor to be far from the blaring noise of blame and disappointment. But the noise followed him in his head, and his thoughts became louder and louder, and deep in the mud, Snee the Sea Snake wriggled and writhed painfully at the bottom of the sea.

That's where the story ended for Taitt.

The nervous breakdown was on a mean countdown. The only question was if it would play out during the ceremony.

Don and Nancy Greene sat, hand in hand, behind my sister and Taitt. Nancy dabbed at tears, mainly because she felt she had to, but a few sincere tears were shed over cursing me for being late for my own birthday party and calling me an asshole for making her roast dry. She wondered who Alice was screwing, based on all those phony tears of hers. She wondered what Alice might buy with all that insurance money. *How the hell am I going to come into a million just like that?* she wondered. She speculated on the cost of flights to Hawaii this time of year. She wondered how many Air Miles points Don had racked up and how many he'd be willing to part with to get her there. She wondered if she'd rather have a diamond tennis bracelet or a new watch, since things were sure to go on sale at my store. She wondered why the little twat who did her nails at the salon pushed the bubble gum colour on her when it wasn't really the colour of bubble gum at all. And then she started picking away the polish so she could go back in, post-funeral, complain, and get the little twat to redo the job with different polish. Those were her words.

Don Greene sat quietly next to her with his arms crossed, wondering why he hadn't made a move on me earlier. *I've wasted the greatest opportunity in life,* he thought. *To tell the one you love that you love them a great deal.* He reviewed all of the moments in which he believed I had given him a sign or a green light. He argued with the voice in his head about those moments, and whether they were false signals or not. He continued to debate the official status of my sexuality, and where I might fall on the spectrum of it all. Undecided, he wondered if it even mattered. Don came to the conclusion that, if propositioned, I would have jumped at the chance, not as an act of homosexuality but simply out of a desire for raw human contact, given my imprisonment of a marriage. He was now more certain than ever that he should have made a move; that he should have just put it out there and gone in for a kiss or an ass grab in my shed and just played jazz from there. He wondered when he would come out to Nancy. Given my death, was this a sign to actively get out there and find a guy?

I did my best not to cause a disturbance when Alice stood next to my processed corpse and attempted her sham of a speech about loss and how we must "all come together" throughout this difficult grieving process. During this speech, many attendees thought her dress was cut inappropriately low on the bustline. My friend, Dan Pizzuto, thought the exact opposite. Dan, who sat next to his pregnant wife, Davida, constructed a vivid fantasy involving a hardcore scene with the grieving widow that turned quite violent near the end. I did not see the choking or face-slapping with bare feet section coming at all. Neither did he, but he went along with it in his mind, and his arteries filled his penis with blood. He wondered what daydreams like this meant. He wondered if he was cut out to be a good husband and father with such thoughts. Moreover, would he go to Hell for managing to boast a massive erection at his friend's funeral? That was a legitimate concern for Dan. He thought about open-heart surgeries, roadkill, and having his fingernails pulled from the quick with pliers. All of this in an attempt to deflate the situation. No such luck.

My uncle Phil had arrived late and spent the entirety of Alice's speech worried about where he had parked. The church parking lot was full, so he left it around back in the reserved spots for the reverend and the choir, exclusively. He had fifty pounds of marijuana in the trunk and was terrified of getting towed. More than that, he was annoyed with the timing of the funeral and that he hadn't been able to deliver his product beforehand. He wondered if his criminal activity was oblivious to the entire family or if he was paranoid, and if he *was* paranoid, should he lay off smoking his own product? You see, Uncle Phil worked day in and day out on the assembly line at the Ford plant in Oakville and was desperate to kiss that life goodbye. As Alice delivered her eulogy, he continued to weigh the pros and cons of his marijuana-dealing side gig. But time and time again, he reached the conclusion that the rewards outstripped the risk. He imagined that jail would be better than the assembly line. He began to sweat profusely. His face ran with salt water, as if an invisible showerhead, piped straight from the ocean, poured down on his head from above.

His wife, Charlene, thought the sweat was due to emotion. She rubbed his arm and grabbed his hand in support. She whispered that she loved him. She meant that with every fibre.

Bob Graham, Bob the Bully, well, he sat in the back row, where bullies instinctively know to sit. He sat there thinking about how he treated me in grade school and high school. He imagined saying sorry to me, but he had a great deal of difficulty doing so, even within the safety of imagination. He saw me taking the apology really well and then asking him to go out for a beer. He said he was too busy, but maybe sometime. He thought that there would never be a sometime to share a beer with me. He just wanted to get the apology off his chest. He thought about the fact that he needed a college degree to apply for a sales job at Snap-On Tools he really wanted. He wondered when he might run out of money. He wondered how he was going to pay for cancer treatments and wondered how people his age could possibly be diagnosed with cancer. He decided it wasn't a bad form of cancer, because it was the skin variety, but he couldn't remember the proper term. He thought it started with an *M*. He sincerely hoped I was getting laid in Heaven, but that was more about men getting laid in Heaven, in general. If the cancer was serious, he wanted Heaven to be about getting laid. He knew that's why suicide bombers did that sort of thing. For the heaven part and the girls, the virgins, and the getting laid, but he couldn't recall for the life of him how many virgins they were promised. Was it ninety-nine or a hundred, or nine hundred?

Lucky bastards, he concluded. *No wonder they're so eager to off themselves.* And then he thought about converting to the Muslim faith just so that he might be able to do the same and get all those virgins. In his mind, he fired an imaginary spitball and hit the casket dead-centre. Hit it so hard, it cracked the wood and would stick there forever to decompose alongside me. *Gotcha one last time, Luke,* he thought.

He smiled.

I smiled too, actually.

. . .

In spite of the facts that my funeral surfaced to me: affairs, criminals, bigots, and a giant helping of overall ignorance, I suppose it didn't matter a grain of sand. None of it mattered at all in context with the Post-Death Line and the lives I had led. I had been male and female thousands of times. Straight and gay and everything in between. Practised every faith and none at all. I had died at birth and lived to be a hundred and six. I had been the best of Samaritans and the worst of criminals.

Honest and deceitful.

Faithful and adulterer.

Murderer and victim.

Wealthy and poor.

Loved and hated.

Leader and follower.

I had seen and done it all.

Bought the T-shirt, as they say.

However, the betrayal of Geoff and Alice continued to linger.

. . .

After the funeral service, I floated alongside my mother down to the church basement for the luncheon catered by my aunt Jean. Everyone lied about how good the sandwiches were. Stories continued to be shared among the guests. All in exaggerated form, of course, and as the stories of praise rolled off tongues, the thoughts that followed only highlighted my many faults. It baffled me why those were not talked about at this event. Those flaws equalled my strengths, didn't they?

What a sad imbalance for celebrating a life.

While people milled about speaking half-truths about me and hating the sandwiches, Taitt Champion had allowed the pending nervous breakdown to bubble over in the parking lot outside the church. Many bore witness to this. Several thought he was taking my death quite hard.

"He really loved Luke," Fran Davidson said while getting into her car.

"Such a shame. Closest thing to a real brother he had," said my friend Adam Wood to his wife, Jane. Of all the onlookers, not a single set of arms remained uncrossed, as if to shield them from what they were witnessing.

The news of Taitt's actions in the parking lot travelled quickly into the church basement, down the hall, into a room, and finally to my sister, who was taking plastic wrap off an assortment of now-stale desserts. When the news registered, she felt herself take one leap and landed in the parking lot seconds later. Everything in between was a blur, she thought. Upon arrival, Brooke did her best to get Taitt from the fetal position, where he rocked back and forth, sporadically kicking and clawing at the pavement, and screaming about a Sea Snake named Snee. After Taitt's mind broke, I couldn't bear witness any longer. Deathly slow as I was, I began floating home to see what Alice might do next.

• • •

Later that afternoon, I watched Alice bag my clothes for charity. She ran through a thousand scenarios for where her life could go from that point forward. It was throughout this process that I could finally determine which clothing she thought looked good on me. The flowered bathing trunks I would have never suspected.

The phone rang and rang all afternoon; people calling with their sympathies. She thanked them for attending the funeral and for bringing food, if they had brought it. She did this while trying on lingerie and looking in the mirror. "It's so sad," she would say to the callers. "It means the world to me that you called. I'll get over it eventually, but it'll take some time." Then, as the caller on the other end continued to alleviate her grief, she would pose into the mirror and push up her breasts or lift the black lace or pull it aside, exposing herself to the mirror, as if attempting to seduce the person looking back at her.

She was grieving only that she had purchased the black and not the red.

. . .

The sun eventually ducked behind the century-old maples, and the doorbell rang. Geoff Black held a bottle of vodka in one hand and sheepishly knocked on the door with the other. The one with his wedding ring. Alice opened the door, and Geoff's mind exploded with imagery of what would transpire. Thoughts Alice seemed to read from him perfectly, which amazed me. A silent transfer of images instructing the forthcoming sequence of events.

Truly remarkable.

Shortly thereafter, she and Geoff came together, but not in grief … in our marital bed. I hovered through the entire thing, buzzing and floating around, as if a different vantage point in the room might be less disturbing. However, every angle provided me with the irrefutable evidence that these two were connected on another level.

Throughout the carnal act I was taking in, Alice seemed hard-wired to Geoff, able to share what she thought and wanted, exactly when she wanted it. In turn, he was able to do the same with her. All without speaking a single word. It was the moment when Alice paused to gather the pillow from my side of the bed in order to place it under her lower back for support, that I came to wonder if this might be common among the living who are perfectly matched spiritual counterparts. And in the category of love and the sub-category lust, my best friend and my wife seemed perfectly matched.

What was originally quite disturbing became a work of art. An act of beauty.

What I felt after that was regret.

Regret that I had never experienced that level of connectivity.

Regret that Alice and I had spent five years on Earth with the wrong person.

Regret that I had failed to seek out my matched spirit — wherever she was hiding in the world. My Diana-of-no-last-name.

When Geoff and Alice eventually finished, they lay on the bed winded and content. Alice proclaimed to God how good it all was, while Geoff searched for an exit strategy from his current wife. Certainly, that was not going to be a lay-up of any kind. Geoff and his wife, Anabelle, shared ownership of a high-end furniture store called Black & Blue. Anabelle's maiden name was Blue; she adopted Geoff's last name when they married. Hence the name of the store and company they were equal partners in. A store by which they were doing exceptionally well, importing luxury furniture from around the world and selling it for a significant markup. I had stood at their wedding and remember when Geoff told me, upon my return from gemology school, that he intended to marry a woman we both knew. "And I don't have to tell you how loaded she is," he said.

Geoff had said this because his family was the opposite of "loaded" and he grew up in a less prestigious area of the city, with his mother and father barely scraping by. His folks spent well beyond their means to ensure that Geoff got into a good school and would be rubbing elbows with children from affluent families. It was their hope that the money would rub off on him somehow and he would become successful through assimilation. Unlike the rest of our classmates, Geoff's confidence had nothing to do with the bank balance of his parents. Geoff excelled in a category that couldn't be bought or taught: good looks. Unfairly so, actually. That was the only hammer in his toolkit, and Geoff got by with it his entire life.

By grade ten, he had been approached by an agent when walking through the mall with his mom. Soon after that, Geoff was a full-blown model and his image began popping up on billboards, in magazines and catalogues. Every so often, he would miss school for a few days here and there because he had booked work in New York and Milan for fashion shoots, or to walk a runway into an ocean of flashing lights. Geoff, he was the real deal, but he didn't let it go to his head. He knew where he was from. He knew he wasn't like the kids he went to school with. Geoff became the guy who rich girls wanted to "slum it" with, as he put it.

"These girls love to mess around with me, but they'd never marry me," he would say. "I don't have the million-dollar family or the prestige to marry one of these stuck-up zombies." With the money he made modelling, Geoff helped his parents carry the financial load and began to chip away at the mountain of debt they had undertaken. "The women, they make all the real money in modelling," he said. "But it feels good to help my folks out." Thus, nothing much changed for Geoff financially. He understood that fifty grand or a hundred grand wasn't going to change the social status of his parents.

All he wanted were my smarts and last name. All I wanted was to be him.

During weekend sleepovers, we would howl with laughter as he acted out situations from class, as if he were one of the many stuck-up zombies. This usually led to one of his characters wrestling me to the ground, demanding a marriage proposal and a piece of my father's real-estate holdings, or she would eat my brains. Geoff and I were best buds, and we didn't care that we came from different upbringings and lifestyles. We were best friends because we had fun and because we were loyal to one another. One night, when we were camping out in the backyard, he told me that I was the best kind of person in the world. He said I was a like a unicorn or something, a rich kid with a poor kid's disposition. And that's why we were able to be best friends.

Fast forward ten years.

When he told me that he had found the woman he intended to marry, I can't say I was on board one hundred percent. In an ironic twist, this woman was Anabelle, and she was one of the stuck-up zombies from our high school graduating class. She was the zombie he would mimic the most during our sleepovers years past. She was the one pinning me down and eating my brains.

"Her old man thinks I could be a good salesman, so he's going to give us seed money to start a furniture business. Ultra high-end," he said.

"Annabelle?" I said.

"She's changed. Trust me."

I disagreed and voiced my concern.

Somehow, he convinced me to stand at their wedding as his best man, because that's what loyal friends do. No, Geoff, loyal friends say something when they think their closest friend is doing something insane and incorrect. He promptly told me to shut up and stop that kind of talk, so I took a front row seat for the impending train wreck as his best man and best friend. Best friends are first responders to the scene, ready to pick up the pieces when all of the rail cars fold into each other, open up like torn pop cans, and leave a swath of destruction a mile long. I was that friend. I was ready, but contrary to my prediction, no train wreck took place.

The truth was, Anabelle had, in fact, changed. She had become a really lovely and warm person, and we became good friends over the years. The unfortunate truth was that my ever-loyal best friend fell dangerously in love with his new money and lifestyle and showed signs of becoming an entitled zombie himself. The infection was in there; it was just a matter of time. Years passed, and we drifted apart as friends. When we were able to get the four of us together for a barbecue, he connected with Alice better than he connected with me. Not that I thought much of it at the start. But as he began to pull away from me, I saw less and less of him as Alice (unbeknownst to me) was seeing more and more.

"You're thinking about Anabelle again," said Alice, still winded from the athletic entanglement.

"I am."

"I know it sounds horrible, especially on this day, but I feel like God removed Luke from the equation as a sign," suggested Alice.

"A sign of what?"

"That we need to be together."

"I want to be clear here. God killed Luke for us, is that what you're saying?"

"I prefaced it with 'I know it sounds horrible....'"

"That doesn't make it less horrible."

"Forget the God part. Look, I think it was a sign. We need to act on it. Life is too short."

"I just buried my best friend. I don't need this right now."

"But what? You needed *this*? What we just did right here after the funeral using his pillow to support my lumbar?" she said and hit him in the chest with it. "You needed that, but you can't talk to me about our future, post–Luke Stevenson?"

Geoff said nothing. He simply stared at the ceiling. His thoughts were about being trapped in quicksand — sinking and sinking and sinking, until only his fingers were visible, still attempting to grasp at something for safety. Then both Anabelle and Alice entered his daydream, attempting to rescue him. The women dove head first into the quicksand after him until only their four kicking legs were visible. The kicking legs stopped. Twitched. Then flopped awkwardly from their hinges at the knees.

Geoff snapped out of it and sat up in bed, sweating.

"What's the matter with you?" said Alice.

"Just relax on all that stuff for now," he said. "It will all happen sooner or later."

"On your clock, Geoff. Whenever you feel like it," she said, rolled over, and clicked off the light on the bedside table. The antique knock-off Tiffany lamp that I had purchased for her because Nancy Greene had one just like it, except not quite as good.

• • •

At this low point, I thought it best to contact my Mentor Spirit. The rules stated I had twenty-four hours to do so, but feeling all of this new power and not knowing how to access it was frustrating.

I needed the advice of a veteran.

I needed the means to satisfy the second reason for returning to Earth after death: to identify the location and well-being of Diana-of-no-last name.

5

The Bookkeeper had armed me with instructions on how to contact my Mentor. I projected the desire to meet the spirit, and Robert F. Sutherland appeared to me seconds later. However, I could sense an awkward vibration.

"Luke James Stevenson?"

"Yes. You must be Robert."

"Rob is fine."

And we shared our respective histories within seconds. Rob, a young tobacco farmer from Farmington, North Carolina, near Winston-Salem, was ended not by smoking his own product but by the hand of an angry neighbour after coming into ownership of the massive family farm at only nineteen years of age.

Rob ran through my story, which I had uploaded to him.

"Sorry about the accident, kid. Damn shame, if you ask me."

"Oh, it's fine."

"How's the wife taking it?" he said, and then I shared with him the clip of Alice and Geoff Black, post-funeral. "Yup," he said. "Seen that before."

His vibration increased. "Look, I'm here for you one hundred percent, Luke, but can you do me a helluva favour?"

"Happy to."

"Fantastic. I owe you one. First lesson — travel. I want you to imagine your form coming in on itself, condensing, if you will. When you feel a slight shock, I want you to quickly project the desire to visit an exact location." He shared with me an exact location.

I didn't question. I just did it. Focused.

I felt my form come in on itself, felt the shock, and projected the requested destination. In an immeasurably short amount of time, we both arrived in a living room in Tunja, Colombia. Thousands of miles were travelled in a fraction of a second. And there we were, hovering over a fortysomething woman seated in a wooden rocking chair.

This was game-changing.

I could see the world. Go anywhere.

Be anywhere in seconds of manifesting the desire and location. At that very moment, I thought that the ghost "buddy-system" was going to work out just fine, and for the first time since delivery, I recall being excited about my predicament.

"Close call, kid!" he said. "I really didn't want to miss this. I've been tracking this channel for months now. Thanks for playing ball and tagging along so quick."

"No problem," I said. "But why are we here?"

Carmen, the woman, the one in the rocking chair, had become fed up with the years of ongoing battery on account of her husband and had been planning her escape for months. As it happened, I had arrived on escape day.

"It's like a whole goddamn world of reality TV, Luke. In the form we're in, you just have to choose the channels you want to watch, sit back, and enjoy."

"Channels?"

"Well, yeah, I call people's lives 'channels' 'cause that's how you have to treat them. And with our gift of travel, you can flip from one to the other with ease. Some people's lives, you know, you just get all caught up in. Don't get bogged down on just one. You have to keep flipping. Lucky for you, you're here for the climax of this dandy. Trust me, friend. This'll be one for the ages."

By the time Rob had finished with the detailed preamble to the story, the husband had arrived home from work, and Carmen welcomed him with a three-ounce gin martini.

Three olives.

And a layer of ice chips floating on top, like having been broken up by a barge.

Before handing it over, she eyeballed him while taking a huge sip from it herself. He had no suspicion of it, but she did this to dispel any thoughts of poisoning. Poisoning hadn't crossed his mind. But he did find it rather strange. Never before had Carmen participated in his alcoholism to this degree. Never had she been there to so actively offer it up on a platter and fuel a forthcoming beating.

Never had she been so bold.

As Rob had explained, the white-collar coward was used to hunting for his wife, finding her in different nooks of the house, cowering and whimpering.

"It's like a version of hide-and-go-seek, but with a shit-kicking at the end," said Rob. "She used to hide and pray to God that he wouldn't find her. Only one day she realized God wasn't listening or didn't care, so she set out to do something about it." Carmen stroked the stubble on his face and loosened his navy blue spotted tie.

"I'll be in the in the bedroom. Hiding," said Carmen. "Get as drunk as you want."

What was this but an outright act of war? It was something that couldn't be tolerated. He decided that due to this strange display of confidence and challenge to his authority, today's beating would be particularly harsh. He wondered how he could get away with taking it up a notch and not have her end up in the hospital like that one time. Too risky. His mind pulsed with creativity.

Two hours later, after exactly 412 millilitres of gin, he made his way to the bedroom and knocked on the closed door. He knocked three times. Then six times. The knocking increased in both volume and intensity. He tried to turn the handle and found that the door had been locked.

"Carmen, what have I said about locked doors in my house?" he said. "Unlock it! Unlock it immediately!"

"No," said Carmen. "I don't feel like it."

The husband became enraged. He paced outside the door like a lion behind bars awaiting a meal. When the hunger became too great, the value of the door became meaningless. Kick after kick after kick at the door as he swore up and down.

"You're going to need a crowbar, you idiot," said Carmen. "There's one in the shed beside the tire pump."

"When I come back with the crowbar, Carmen," he said, attempting to catch his breath. "It's headed your direction."

"I was hoping you'd say that!" she said. "Yes, certainly with the crowbar!"

He made his way to the shed and located the crowbar. It was exactly where Carmen had said it would be. In fact, she had placed a Christmas bow on it and a card with the lipstick imprint of a kiss. He ripped off the card and bow and wondered if Carmen would make it out of this beating alive. He was no longer so concerned about a trip to the hospital. *There's no way around that now*, he thought.

Minutes later, he slammed the end of the crowbar in the doorjamb and began to pry. The wood frame moaned before cracking and splintering.

"It's working! Keep going!" she screamed, now clapping with encouragement.

When the crowbar had applied enough torque, the door popped open.

Red with fury and dripping with sweat, he entered the room and found Carmen sitting on the bed drinking a glass of red wine, along with her three brothers, all having done some previous drinking of their own — equally as fortified with courage and conviction.

These brothers were armed with the following: a bat, some rubber tubing, and a hacksaw. The tallest brother closed the door behind the bewildered husband and suggested that he drop the crowbar. Carmen walked over and picked it up off the floor. She walked back to the bed and suggested that her siblings get to work.

They did.

Some time passed.

The three brothers left the barrel-chested spousal abuser with eyes swollen, ribs broken, and hands missing. The rubber tubing provided tourniquet bracelets.

"There go your punching days," said the smallest brother, wiping blood off the hacksaw with a facecloth.

"Your drinking days too," said the middle brother.

"Maybe with a straw or something, but you'll need to find someone to pour," said the tallest brother. "Call me, I'll come over. Anytime."

All the brothers laughed.

Rob laughed harder. He found great entertainment in all of this.

"This is just downright amazing," said Rob. "Don't you think, pal? Wow, what an ending."

I gave off some sort of uncomfortable vibration, and he teased me about it throughout the cleanup of the blood and the conversation about how to dispose of the hands.

Yes, what to do with the hands, indeed.

The smallest brother, the one with the crucifix and barbed wire tattoo on his forearm, suggested making gloves out of them, and Rob laughed so hard, the lights flickered. The brothers packed up Carmen's core belongings and placed the cordless telephone beside the panicked husband. The middle brother suggested he dial for help. This prompted more laughter, and one final kick to the abuser's ribs was dealt. A proper kick. Something a professional goalkeeper would have been proud of.

Carmen asked for a moment alone with her husband. The brothers left the room, but not before a few parting words of their own. She knelt down beside his face. Their eyes met.

"Please," he said. "I need help. I need you to call an ambulance, or I'll die."

"Why should you be saved?"

"I love you, Carmen," he said. "You can't leave me like this."

"You're right. I can't. It wouldn't be right."

Carmen grabbed the infamous crowbar and with one swing buried the hooked end in his neck. His eyes rolled around, and he gurgled for a bit.

With a cloth, she wiped her prints from the crowbar, now a permanent fixture in his body. She calmly walked to the door and softly closed it behind her, as if not to wake a sleeping baby.

The husband lay alone with seconds to live. In his mind, he cried for God to help him. He praised the Lord and begged for mercy. He begged for Jesus to take him to Heaven.

Then his squirming and gurgling came to an end.

He was surely standing at the back of the Post-Death Line, and many thousands of the recently deceased were about to upload and experience the life of a drunken spousal abuser from Tunja, Colombia. All would share his death in the same horrific fashion.

"Show's over, kid," said Rob. "That turned out better than expected, I gotta say." And then I downloaded from him what he had expected to take place, which was equally as disturbing.

"Any questions for me at this time?"

"I can't really think of any, no."

"I'll tell you this, kid. We all chose wrong. Us ghosts, we all really botched it opting to come back to this hellhole. Here we are, armed with all the knowledge and perspective the Post-Death Line gives us, but we remain invisible and unable to do shit, save for flickering lights or raising the hair on the backs of necks. Just all bullshit, bush-league stuff. A bunch of onlookers is all we are. An army of peeping Toms."

"Sounds terrible," I said.

"Torture if you let it be. Don't get sucked into the really bad channels. Ghosts can get consumed. They become pain junkies and only hover around the worst of humanity."

"I'll try to steer clear."

"Listen, after you get your feet wet with travel and latch on to a few channels, you'll find a hobby. That's what I suggest. Motorsports is mine. Has been for forty years now. I take in every motorsport race, practice, and time trial the world has to offer."

"I really like music," I said.

"Now you have the best seats in the house!"

"I guess I do."

"Also, you're still basically human. Don't beat yourself up too bad when you fall victim to an emotion. There's nothing you can do about it. Don't try to reason your way out. It's a pit."

"Show me how to do those small-time stunts, would you?" I asked.

He sent me over the image of a movie poster for a recent Hollywood blockbuster titled *Happy to Oblige*. The poster featured a heavily muscled action hero as he fired a machine gun while screaming into the desert. Then Rob proceeded to show me some tricks. They were easier than I thought.

"And how would I go about finding someone?"

"Who?"

"Diana."

"What's her last name?"

"I don't know."

"You don't know."

"Correct. But I think she could be somewhere in Ontario."

He sent me the image of a haystack. Then a needle glowed and throbbed from inside it, as to identify itself.

"Here's how we find the needles," he said, and so went the lesson on geo-location. Essentially, this is how I found her:

I was able to filter and batch all of the thought patterns with respect to the name Diana within the geographic boundaries of Ontario, Canada. From there, I was able to filter out the toddlers, teens, young adults, and the elderly, which left me only 643 to visit personally.

I visited 333 before I was brought to a bungalow in Burlington.

And there she was: Diana-of-no-last-name, gently rocking a swaddled newborn in a turn-of-the-century pine rocker.

She sang a song to the little baby boy.

It went like this:

Mamma's own dear little baby.
Mamma's own dear little boy.
Mamma's own dear little baby.
Mamma's own dear little boy.

The song was repeated over and over and over, regardless of the sleeping status of the child. A man entered the room after thirty minutes or so. He sat down on the floor, unknotted his tie, and unbuttoned the top two mother-of-pearl-looking buttons on his white dress shirt.

I read all of his thought projections.

This was her husband.

A good man, from what I could tell, based on his thoughts, anyway. He just sat there and listened to the song over and over as well. The two of us, both present and equally silent, captured by the wonderment that was the finest woman either of us had ever known. Of course, I was thrilled to see how well Diana-of-no-last name's life had turned out. It made me happy to see her in such a good place.

A safe place. A place of love.

Diana eventually wound down her song to find that both the baby and her husband were fast asleep. She couldn't believe how well life had turned out for her. She wondered how someone who had sold pills and powder to get through school deserved such a happy ending. She wondered how the lives of those she sold pills and powder to had turned out.

Not this good, she thought.

She thought she should thank someone but wasn't sure about God, so she thanked the Universe in general and thought that was a safe bet. She wondered if her parents, who had died when she was a young girl, were looking down on her. She asked for their forgiveness about the pills and powder part but wanted them to see her now.

"Your little girl made it," she whispered.

I could sense no other vibrations in the room, so her parents weren't present. But if no one else heard her, I certainly had. Perhaps I could do something godly. My energy was focused directly at the thick yellow flame of an antique coal oil lamp she had burning close by. I pushed energy toward that flame with everything I had, and it snapped and danced. It billowed black smoke out of the glass chimney.

She smiled. "Thanks, Mom," she said.

And my time there was complete.

Diana was safe. Diana was happy.

And the second mystery had been answered.

At that point, hovering around seemed an intrusion, so I decided that would be the last time I saw Diana.

And I wish that had been the case.

• • •

After Diana, I travelled to the house I was raised in. My mother was dusting the hutch. More specifically, the picture of my high school graduation. She shed a few tears and blew her nose into the dust rag, which resulted in a fit of sneezing. She broke up laughing at herself between sneezes. I laughed as well. Eager to flex what powers I had, I made a log in the nearby fireplace crackle and pop, as if it were a firework, and then focused my form close to her. The hair on her arms and the back of her neck stood on end, and she looked up and said, "Thank you, Luke. I knew you hadn't missed that one," and continued on with her dusting.

. . .

For many months, I wandered. I hovered in lecture halls and concert halls, sports stadiums, art galleries, changerooms, and honeymoon suites. When I was finished with all of that, I became addicted to courtroom drama and hovered over the guilty and innocent alike. It's fascinating to watch legal proceedings when you can tap into the thought patterns of those charged with crimes.

The only one in the room able to access the hard truth.

I did my best to steer clear of the dark matter. Cries of pain clawed at me, inviting me to travel to them, but I resisted. Scenes of murder and torture. Scenes of injustice and human rights violations by the thousands — all there for the viewing, but not for me. I had lived enough of all that first-hand in the Post-Death Line. At this point in my afterlife, I had checked off both reasons for my return.

There was nothing more for me, really.

The truth was, I was ready for What's Next, but my curiosity had managed to cage me on Earth until my Spirit Lease came due. A wave of depression came over my form, and perspective caused me to replay the worst bouts of depression I had experienced in the Post-Death Line.

Fine, perhaps in comparison I wasn't depressed … but I was nothing.

I was flat.

I was ready for something and open to anything.

Within seconds of coming to that realization, I received the call every ghost knows is coming sooner or later.

The Bookkeeper had deemed me ready. A Recently Delivered Spirit, an RDS, had been delivered back to Earth and was paired with me.

She reached out to me within seconds of her arrival. Her name was Safia.

This was the Safia that would go on to change the world, and history thereafter.

6

It's the ghosting equivalent to meeting your unborn child, I suppose. That would be the closest comparison, given that you are paired with another spirit for the remainder of their time or yours. In the Line I had been a mother many thousands of times, so it felt familiar. When the call arrives, it is undeniable. Overtakes your form, entirely. Like an orgasm or electrocution.

Not something to be ignored.

The event is marked by a very distinct whispering. The whisper fills your form and mentions the name of the RDS, paired with coordinates placing the exact location of the new ghost. And off you go.

• • •

It was just after lunch, local time, when I arrived in the small town square in Pakistan. The majestic white-capped mountains surrounding the scene were not majestic enough to distract me from the horror that had transpired. It was all too obvious and grim.

Inescapable.

The only dirt in the square unmarked by the tragedy was located at the centre of the chaos.

A perfect circle bearing unearthed, fresh soil.

From that circle, colours shot out in every direction. From two hundred metres above the world, the scene looked like a human eye, except the flecks of colour surrounding the pupil were made of blood and bone, hair and clothing.

Never had I felt so many vibrations in one place. The event was so fresh that people hadn't yet rushed the scene. Bodies hadn't been cradled and limply rocked by sobbing others. The unconscious hadn't yet woken to discover deep wounds or missing pieces of themselves.

Self-portraits hadn't yet shape-shifted.

The scene just stood still.

The echo of the event still rang in the air, bouncing off the mountings like a grim game of pinball. Dust swirled around bodies, and the vibration of ghosts in attendance increased by the second. Thousands of them. Scream Followers. Ghosts following thought projections of fear from the living. These ghosts, these pain chasers, addicted to human suffering. Travelling from tragedy to tragedy, unable to detach from witnessing the world's horrors. It was something Rob had warned me about many months before. Honestly, this was the first tragic scene I had visited since Carmen and her brothers dealt with her husband. This tragedy in Pakistan, I wouldn't have been there at all if not called there by my RDS.

She hung in the air, and I moved close to her.

I reached out to connect, and the connection was accepted.

"Safia Jaffi," I said.

She responded with a black square housing a red check mark.

I asked to share stories, and we did. I downloaded her life to find that she was a twelve-year-old girl who loved her family, music, and cooking, the older boy down the road, and dancing when no one was looking. At the time of her death, Safia was doing nothing more than waiting her turn at the distribution site to bring some food and supplies home. Doing nothing more than her part. Following orders. Her important familial task for the day. That task, and her life, was interrupted by a teenage boy who was taught to interpret written words differently. Brainwashed to hate.

That boy ran into the centre of a hungry crowd and put an end to thirty-six stories. Those stories stained the earth and soaked into the world to feed crawling things, as all stories do sooner or later, I suppose.

Safia hung there, replaying her life from start to finish, vibrating at the moments of gross untruth. I wasn't able to download the story of the suicide bomber but knew the tune all too well. I had lived the life of a suicide bomber in the Post-Death Line, but in that particular story I had botched the bombing and ended up exploding only myself and my dog well before the detonation site. Like I said, I knew the gist of bomber stories — all carrying similar themes of poverty, deception, brainwashing, and duty.

Safia hung over the gruesome scene, vibrating to a degree I didn't know was possible.

She was angry. No, she was livid.

Beyond livid.

Enraged.

For someone who had recently passed through the Post-Death Line, she shouldn't have been experiencing that degree of rage, but Safia was unequivocally furious. I sent her calming scenes: the Amazon rainforest and thousands of sounds therein, then waves rolling in and out of a pink Bermuda beach.

"Would you like to visit one of those locations, Safia? I can teach you to travel."

She sent me back the image of an asteroid slamming into Earth and shattering it into a billion chunks. The chunks of Earth hung in space and floated among the shape-shifting mercurial pools of blood.

I sent her back the rainforest scene, except this time a python hanging from one of the trees formed the shape of a question mark and asked her why she was so angry.

Here's why: Safia had returned to Earth as a ghost in order to look over her little sister, Haadiya. But moments after she was delivered back, Haadiya died due to injuries suffered in the suicide blast, and Safia was left to hover over her sister's lifeless body in the square. She wished to change her decision immediately, but the Bookkeeper informed her that all decisions were final, sending her the standard digital image of numbers counting down, revealing the remainder of her spiritual lease.

Sixty-one years, two months, fourteen days, nine hours, and ten point seventy-eight seconds.

She sent a requisition to the Bookkeeper for information surrounding the current status and whereabouts of her sister. The Bookkeeper replied, "Status: Required Perspective Achieved. Location: What's Next, as per her decision."

She vibrated with such force that locals took shelter. One local suggested the blast might have set off an earthquake or tremor. Many others agreed.

"Safia, what was that? How did you do that?"

"I feel like I could explode. Have you not felt like that?"

"Once, but perspective took over. Just try to let it pass."

"I can't."

"Use your experiences from the Line. You've felt this level of hurt before."

"I haven't," she said. "That is the problem. The stories in the Line, they all just compounded."

She intercepted a thought projection from another young suicide bomber only a few cities away, about to carry out his misguided orders. She asked me to take her there to prevent it.

But I wouldn't. I couldn't.

"Take me there!" she demanded.

"Why?"

"You're my teacher!"

"It's already too late," I said, and we saw the images and heard the muffled screams. Her form grew swollen with frustration, and the vibrations that followed set off another shaking of the earth.

"There was nothing you could have done," I said. "We're incapable. You need to stop vibrating like that."

"That makes no sense," she said, and I suggested that wasn't the kind of statement a ghost should be making. "If I am chained to this fate, should I not attempt to change things?"

"Humanity has to grow at its own pace," I said. "You know that."

"Let's speed it up."

"Safia, I know this is frustrating, but I need to calm you before you vibrate like that again. Listen, there's nothing we can do to prevent horrible acts, and chasing them to witness the suffering does you no good. Let's go to a waterfall or check out the pyramids. What do you say?"

"I was tricked," she said, and sent me the image of a fox, standing on his hind legs, smoking a cigar. The fox wore white T-shirt that read, "Bookkeeper."

I sent her back a few hundred question marks.

She sent me an image of herself bound and handcuffed to a block of concrete under thirty feet of water. For one reason or another, the Post-Death Line had failed to provide the context required to be a ghost, and I uploaded a form to the Bookkeeper asking him what had gone wrong but got nothing in return.

"If it makes you feel better, I made the wrong choice as well, but we're here now, together. Let me show you some neat things."

She sent me a small video clip of the words "neat things" being rigged with explosives and obliterated.

Fair enough.

When I asked if she wanted to talk, she shared the argument she had with her mother, prior to the attack.

"I refuse to go alone," she said.

"Safia, I need your sister's help here, today," said her mother.

"If you want more supplies, I need more hands," she said.

"Not this time. You must go alone and do your part. As much as you can carry and come straight home."

"Do you really expect me to carry enough? With these arms?" she said. And then Safia outstretched her thin arms in an attempt to reveal their inadequacy. Her mother threw up arms of her own. Up, up into the air, and ordered Haadiya to accompany Safia, after all. The mother said, "Be a good girl along the way."

And her little sister was a good girl along the way. She was a good girl while they waited their turn to reach the supply truck. While the people yelled.

And pushed.

While arms were reaching and people were sweating.

Eventually, Safia made it to the front and grabbed supply bag after supply bag, stacking them on top of her sister's outstretched arms. Enough bags to cover up her face and permanent fixture of a smile. Enough bags to mute her laugher.

Safia giggled.

She had successfully loaded down her mule of a little sister and reached back for two more bags for herself.

"Come now, Haadiya," she said. "Let's see if you can keep up with me."

Then she turned and saw the handsome teenage boy run into the crowd and loudly scream. Heartbeats froze and goose bumps formed on everyone in attendance. Fear removed screams from their open mouths, and then came the blast. Hot air pushed metal quickly through the crowd.

And then Safia was all the way back to the beginning, telling her mother she refused to go to the distribution site without her sister. I watched the scene play out in its entirety the 410 times she ordered it to.

Hovering beside her. Doing my best to help. Doing my worst to do so.

By this time the square had filled with people. The dead were dragged into rows, and a whole lot of pictures were taken of them. An American correspondent spoke in front of a camera and tried to recap the tragic incident to the world but thought more about the amount of grit in the wind that day and what it was doing to her face and hair. That if some of the grit got into her mouth would it damage her enamel? It was at this point that I saw Safia project her desire for a much-required change in scenery.

"Would you like me to teach you how to travel now?" I suggested.

She accepted.

• • •

We made it in time to see the sun set at Rick's Cafe in Jamaica and just hung there until it was seconds from over. We hovered above the honeymooners, vacationers, and locals who never grew tired of taking in the awe-inspiring sunset. Even the heavily muscled high divers couldn't compete with Mother Nature's feature presentation. The sun touched the ocean and began its transformation into a blood orange.

Safia, still enraged, was unarmed against its beauty, and for a moment was at ease. "Pretty," she said.

"I thought you'd like it." The sun disappeared into the vast ocean, and night fell on Rick's Cafe.

"I was tricked," said Safia, and she uploaded to me her interaction with the Bookkeeper. I watched it play out.

"I see you asked if your sister was alive," I said. "That was true at the time of the question. She was indeed alive."

"Yes, she was alive, but she was in the process of dying."

"The Bookkeeper answered your question."

"My sister's condition at the time of the question was critically important to my decision-making."

"Then perhaps you should have crafted your question differently," I said and shared with her a dozen variances of the question that might have surfaced the response she was looking for.

"I should be in What's Next with my sister. I should be rid of this disgusting planet."

"There are many wonderful things to see. You'll have the time of your afterlife. I'll see to it, personally."

But she identified the shred of doubt that underscored my sentiment and sent me back the image of a donkey braying wildly. The brand on the donkey's ass read, "Luke." I sent her back a smile. She sent me back a horribly disfigured smile, as if it had been badly burned in a fire.

"Safia, I don't think you're supposed to be this angry."

"I have never been so angry," she said, and the earth shook. Bits of rock crumbled from the cliffs at Rick's Cafe. Everyone fled the scene. Rob hadn't taught me to make the earth shake, and for Safia, this was becoming commonplace.

"How do you do that? You have to show me."

"I will not be fine here, Luke," she said and sent me a picture of the ocean labelled, "tears." At the bottom of the ocean was an ivory envelope with my name on it. Inside it was a card. The card read, "I promise."

She promised that if the Bookkeeper was going to bind her to Earth for a decision made with misinformation, she was going to do more than float around. She promised that she was going to make grand changes to the world, no matter what it took.

Every amount of energy in my spiritual composition believed her.

Every bit of me knew that my afterlife was in for a dramatic change.

7

Twenty-four hours later, Safia reached out to me and provided the coordinates of her location. It was the surface of the moon. I sent her back a pencil-drawn man scratching his head. The text read "Is that even possible?" She sent me back a passport with the projection path on how to access the moon.

Off to the moon I went.

We hovered over the Sea of Tranquility, above the peaks of the surrounding lunar mountains, looking down on the stunning blue marble that is Earth.

"I had no idea we could travel to the moon," I said. "This is an incredible view."

"Why didn't you think we could travel here?"

"In the handbook it says that we are tied to Earth," I said. "I guess the moon somehow qualifies."

"You just didn't think to try," she said.

"I guess not."

Safia glowed and vibrated with excitement to my response. She shook the Sea of Tranquility, and a section of surrounding mountain crumbled, broke up, and thundered down into the full depth of the crater.

"I believe we are capable of a lot more than the *Handbook* tells us," she said. I floated away to hover over the Sea of Crises. She promptly followed.

"What's the matter?"

"You shouldn't be talking this way."

"What way should I be talking?"

"I'd rather not be on the moon, to be honest. It feels like we're out of bounds," I said. "I'm leaving."

She sent me a stop sign. I sent back the stop sign riddled with bullet holes.

"If you leave, I will call you back, and if you recall the Rules of Mentorship, that is exactly what you will have to do," she said and sent me a Golden Retriever with its tail between its legs. The Retriever then lay down beside its water bowl, resting its head on its paws. The name on the dog's collar read, "Luke."

"It bothers me that you make everything shake. The Earth and the Moon and make things crumble and break apart."

"Why does that bother you?"

"And the things you say bother me as well. I need to get you cooled down," I said and sent her video clips of professional athletes sitting down into tubs of ice to speed the recovery of their aching muscles. She moved closer to me.

I felt warmth.

That was noteworthy, because I hadn't felt any kind of temperature since I had returned as a ghost. But I felt warmth with her hovering that close to me. Later on, I would learn that this was due to her unique vibration pattern. The same pattern that made the earth shake and would soon end lives.

"What do you see when you look down on Earth, Luke?"

"I see a miracle."

"Continue."

"I see a thing of wonder, where creation and life exists," I said. Immediately, I second-guessed my response. I mean, after having lived the lives of many high scholars, I should have come up with something more eloquent than that. More poetic. Safia assured me that my response wasn't being adjudicated.

"What do you see?" I said.

"I see a place of destruction and death. I see an entirely miserable place where somehow, over a long period of time, the wrong species managed to take control of the planet, poison it, abuse it, and butcher itself in the process. All of this to a degree that warrants severe interference of some kind."

For the first time in my afterlife, I was experiencing fear. Safia could sense it. It was written all over my vibrational composition, but Safia forged ahead with her thoughts.

"My sister and I died in a square because someone else thought it was their duty and responsibility to interfere with the greatest gift on Earth: life."

"I understand."

"Luke, you were a mother in the Post-Death Line. Do you think mothers risk their lives in childbirth, suffer through the delivery of that child, then care for that child with all of their energy and resources, just to see that child ripped apart by bullets or the blade of a machete? Or raped? Tortured or beaten? Blown apart by a bomb? Do you think mothers go to all that trouble to have it end like that?"

"I experienced the Line, Safia. I understand all of this."

"Forget the Line. The Line did nothing but amplify my anger. And the Line is not my point."

"I'm terribly unclear as to your point."

"My point is this: What if I could prevent it?"

"Prevent what?"

"Murder. Violent crimes. What if I could stop it?"

"We can't interfere. You know the rules."

"What if we can?"

"We can't."

"Before travelling to the Moon, you would have been convinced that hovering here was not possible. Am I wrong there?"

Yes, she had me on that point.

"Luke, we've only been told we can't, but I did something recently that has me wondering," she said and uploaded to me an encounter from only a few hours before our conversation on the surface of the moon.

Safia had followed the fear projections of a young woman in Miami, Florida, who, upon walking home from the gym, had refused the advances of a man many years her senior. This guy had pulled up beside her in a complete shitbox of a 1984 Caprice Classic. Both the condition of the car and the condition of the man suggested that they had seen a hard go of it in the world.

Both required maintenance.

The man called out to her a number of times, asking her name and where she was headed. The young girl ignored him, as a young girl would in this situation. In so many words, the man suggested that she shouldn't wear tight clothing if she didn't want the attention. The young woman responded that walking home from the gym in gym clothing wasn't inappropriate and that she wasn't asking for anything at all, except to walk home without being interrupted.

"So, you're going home," said the man.

"Maybe not," said the woman. "Maybe I take a detour by the police station and report you."

The man stated very clearly that he knew she wanted it. The woman disagreed. He said she was giving off signals, and she promptly disagreed again. He said her mouth was saying no but her ass was saying yes, and she picked up her pace a little as her heart rate doubled. Her eardrums pounded due to increased blood pressure. Tears hung from the bottom lids of her eyes. She did her best to remain strong and not to look half as frightened as she was. She prayed to God that the man would just go away. If he did, she would go to church more, and it would be a sign from Jesus that he was looking after her.

After a few more failed attempts to aggressively woo her into his Caprice Classic, the man hurled a slew of insults her direction and finally said farewell. He slowed his car down to a crawl, and the young woman walked on, thinking she was now in the clear. Her eyeballs flicked up to the sky, and she thanked God for what had transpired. She decided, then and there, that Jesus was real and that she would cancel the coffee with her friend Wendy on Sunday morning and would go to church instead, just as she had promised.

This event had to happen, she thought.

This is the sign I've been looking for, she thought.

Things are looking up, she thought.

That was until she heard the roar of the engine and was struck by the vehicle from behind. The back of her head bent the metal of the hood. Her broken body flew off the cracked windshield and onto the patch of manicured grass lining the sidewalk. A sprinkler system set up to water the flawless lawn did its best to wash the blood from her face. Then, by its nature, it left to fulfill its duty elsewhere. However, it would return, and return again.

The man introduced the pedal to the floor mat, and the shitbox sped off.

What's one more dent? he thought.

What's more cracks in the windshield? he thought.

I'm long gone, and in the clear, he thought.

Safia's form became swollen with rage, the earth began to shake so hard the sidewalk cracked, and some of the young woman's blood found its way into those fresh nooks and crannies in the cement. Safia attempted to connect with the young girl but was unable to. There were no more thought projections to be shared. She was gone.

Safia boiled.

In attempting to understand where the assailant was headed, Safia reconnected with him. However, as soon as the connection was made, his body fell limp and his face hit the steering wheel. He slumped into the seat of the Caprice Classic, bleeding profusely from his eyes, ears, and nose. The speeding car eventually came to a stop on account of a light standard.

Sparks met gasoline, and the car exploded.

Dead as a doornail, as they say, making all kinds of a mess from his face as the old velour seat soaked that goop up as best as it could.

He just lay there, nothing more than a fuel source for the oncoming flames.

Safia stopped the upload. "Luke, this sounds crazy, but I believe that when I focused my energy his direction in an attempt to connect with his thoughts, enraged as I was, I inadvertently caused a massive brain aneurysm or hemorrhage of some kind due to my vibration pattern."

"You believe you killed him."

"From the evidence put before you, what is your conclusion?"

"You believe you altered what was meant to be?"

"It looks that way."

"Impossible."

"Why impossible? It happened, did it not?"

She offered to play the scene for me again, but I refused to accept the upload.

"It was an accident," she said. "But nothing happened to me on account of my actions. The rules of ghosting, as stated, had clearly been broken, but nothing happened. Not a message from the Bookkeeper. Not a punishment. Luke, listen to me … nothing."

"It was a wild coincidence. Nothing more. His lease was up," I said, trying my best to rationalize a situation that was causing me to pulse with fear. "Yes, his lease was up at the very second you connected with him, and he was always supposed to die from a horrible brain aneurysm after striking a young woman with his car."

"Interesting hypothesis, Luke," she said, and then sent me the sound of an obnoxiously loud horn used in hockey to signify the end of the period or game. The sound lasted exactly forty-six seconds, so in this case the extended hockey horn was clearly meant to signify sarcasm.

"Play along for a second. Let's say it was me," she said.

"Sure. Let's say you killed him."

"Good. Now, if that is true, let's get back to the question at hand. What if I could prevent acts of violence before they happened?"

"I'm not following," I said, but she knew I was following and called me on it. To say I was thoroughly embarrassed would be an understatement.

"What if I could have melted his brain before he committed the crime?"

"I don't like this already," I said and sent her a cease and desist order, signed and dated at the bottom.

"It gets better."

"Safia, please stop."

"Listen, I can read his mind, as we all can. Ghosts, I mean. But I have played back the situation a million or more times since it happened, and it seems that I can pinpoint the exact moment he decided he was going to do it; that point of no return when he was going to hit her with his car and nothing was going to stop him. There was a discernible moment in his thought pattern, a Thought Marker."

"A Thought Marker."

"It signals the point of no return for human action," she said. "I've been watching violent crimes play out since this incident in Miami, and what I've learned from this research is that I can truly identify the moment of clear choice, the Thought Marker, the moment when there is no turning back in the mind of the assailant."

"Safia, please listen to me."

"What if, after identifying the Thought Marker, I disconnect from the assailant, gather my anger, and throw every bit of vibration energy I have into reconnecting? If this action causes the blood vessels of the human brain to burst, like I believe it can, then I could effectively ..."

"You could effectively prevent murder."

"More than just murder. I could prevent rape, torture, beatings, maiming … you name it. I could prevent acts of violent crime all over the world."

"Safia, I'm not comfortable with this at all," I said, and I sent her certificate of authenticity with regard to that statement.

"Do you want to save lives or just float around like an idiot?"

"That's an unfair question, because that is not our role here as ghosts. We're not some invisible police force. Some invisible army that dispenses capital punishment based on your ability to identify Thought Markers."

"You say we are not, but we could be."

"I can't do what you do, Safia. I can't shake the earth like you can. I can't push energy like you can. I don't share in your rage, and I think we need to seek help from the Bookkeeper on that front. I'm seriously failing as a Mentor here."

Her composition became swollen, and she connected to the entire world at once, taking in every thought. She batched and organized the thoughts into columns, given their varying degrees of violent thought up to and including having just committed a violent crime. I asked how she did that, and she showed me.

"It's important that you know how to do this."

"Why?" I said.

"For later," she said. "When I require your help."

"Safia, I want no part of this. I've made that clear."

"Twelve people were just murdered and sixty-one raped in the last ten seconds. We could have potentially done something."

"Safia, I would like to leave. Please don't call me back if I do."

"This will change the world! Let's do this together! I need you, Luke."

"This is none of our business!" I sent her the cartoon clip of a pit bull barking those words to her at close range, fangs exposed. Hurling long strings of saliva.

This was my first unbridled brush with anger since returning as a ghost, and after coming to grips with my outburst, I was ready to resign my post. It had become all too clear that Safia was too much ghost for me.

All would be mended in my afterlife, if I could just have someone else assigned to me. One who might want to catch an interesting play or a ballgame. One who might want to explore the great mountain ranges of Earth, take in a concert, hover in courtrooms, or float above lovers in honeymoon suites.

Yes, that was exactly the kind of RDS I wished for.

My mind was made up, and I was just about to submit a formal request for a change of RDS to the Bookkeeper, signed and dated, when Safia said, "Would you be willing to change your tune if it meant saving the life of your beloved Diana?"

8

Calvin Handler was the kind of guy you warn your children about. The kind of guy whose abusive upbringing created a filter for his view on the world. A filter that led to his concern for the well-being of others being on par with what he felt for vermin. And Calvin Handler looked the part too.

Tall, but not too tall.

Lanky.

Tight, as if his skin had been shrink-wrapped around his sinewy muscles and protruding vasculature.

An Adam's apple too big for his throat kind of guy.

A greasy, shoulder-length hair tucked behind his ears kind of guy.

A wispy facial hair and dark sunken eyes kind of guy.

You know Calvin Handler. We all do.

We've met him in the street and seen his mug on TV when they show the police sketch artist's rendition of the suspect. He's every bit the character you'd look away from if he met your eyes on the streetcar or subway. If you passed him on the street, you'd pick up your pace without knowing, instinctively wanting to distance yourself from him, as though you might catch something, or worse, that he might catch you.

Calvin Handler is no mystery. He's as dangerous as he looks. Yet people find Calvin. In fact, people flock to him.

And of course, Calvin finds people.

Through this process of being sought out and locating others, he is able to survive in the world, selling pills and powder to people and discarding those who get in his way.

In the case of Diana-of-no-last-name, when she heard from a friend of a friend that she could likely pay for the entirety of her college tuition via selling Calvin's product at school, she thought that was a no-brainer. Who else was going pay for her schooling? And bartending kept you up all hours and unable to study. Pills and powder seemed easy to sell. There was never any shortage of rebellious students who were into experimentation. And experimentation leads to once a weekend, which leads to several times a week, which leads to a habit — and then you have yourself a good old-fashioned customer base.

Game on.

I'll back up a bit. Diana was introduced to Calvin, who made a deal with Diana, and before either of them could say Massassauga Rattler, Diana was his highest-earning wholesaler of pills and powder.

Four years flew by, leaving Diana with an undergrad degree in English and Calvin Handler with a fat wallet. By nature, it also left him eager to continue their business relationship and on-campus empire they had built.

The problem was this: Diana was finished.

After four years, the guilt had taken its toll, and she was ready to carve out a new life. This brings us back to Calvin Handler and how little he valued the lives, dreams, and general well-being of others. So Calvin did what Calvin did and threatened the life of Diana should she choose to discontinue the highly profitable operation they had going. Diana chalked that threat up to the rantings of a miserable, drugged-out lowlife and moved away for teacher's college. But Diana was not easily replaced.

Calvin and I agreed on that.

Flash forward several years, and Diana makes the *Burlington Gazette* as she's captured giving the English Award to her top student, Amanda Grier. What should never be overlooked when discussing characters like Calvin Handler is the reach these creatures have.

Tentacles and eyeballs everywhere. In every city and every town.

And one of his associate eyeballs spotted this picture of Diana in the *Gazette*, clipped it out, and brought it to him personally.

Calvin's version of the story played out several times in his head as he sat in a parked car a few blocks from Diana's house. Safia shared with me Diana's version as we hovered over the 1991 Ford Mustang. And not the five-litre V8 Mustang, I should mention. The lesser Mustang they sold that year with the sewing-machine engine that still looked like a Mustang, but without the pep or price tag.

"What brought you to Diana in the first place?" I said.

"Her story resonated with me when I uploaded your life story, so I wanted to find her. When I did, she was thinking about college and Calvin Handler and what rock he might be hiding under. I did some more digging and located Calvin, just as he had come across the newspaper article and began making plans to kill her."

"Which brings us to now," I said.

"Precisely."

"We can't be sure he's going to kill her."

"I agree. We can't be certain until the Thought Marker presents itself. Then there is no turning back."

"And you haven't seen it yet. For sure."

"He could get into the house and then change his mind. Time will tell. But I need to know if you are with me on this path of violent crime prevention. If you are, we can start with Diana's forthcoming assassin and go from there to make the world a better place."

As she said this, Calvin Handler screwed the silencer onto his revolver with gloved hands. He began to rehearse what he might say when face to face with Diana. A few of his natural choices were:

"Well, well, well … lookie what we have here."

"Well, if it isn't my little Diana banana."

"Hi there, Diana. Miss me? I sure missed you."

"Looks like you called my bluff and lost."

Calvin liked options one and three. He thought two was a little too jovial for the situation at hand and four was out of a bad movie.

We followed him out of the car and toward the house. He picked the lock on the front door as easily as one might remove the steel cage from around the cork on a bottle of champagne. Earlier that afternoon, Calvin had already scouted the house for any telltale signs of an alarm system and saw nothing to be worried about. No contacts on the windows or anything. He wondered why people in nice neighbourhoods tended to skip that expense. He thought it couldn't be a money issue due to the property values. Thus, he concluded that maybe such people decided against alarm systems out of a desire to reflect the safety their neighbourhood. When the lock released, Calvin drew his gun and gently opened the door, turned, and closed it with equal care.

Safia began to vibrate. Calvin thought someone had left the dryer on or something as the walls began to shake.

"Luke, I need to know what to do here. Are you with me in this, or not?"

"This is wrong. This is not our purpose," I said and pulsed again with fear.

Calvin crept up the stairs to the top floor. By now the family wire-haired fox terrier had caught his scent and heard the footsteps, the creak of the stair boards fighting with century-old nails. The terrier began to bark and squared off with Calvin in the hallway. Calvin flicked on the hall light and made short work of the family pet. Two pops and the terrier staggered into the doorframe of the master bedroom and began the process of bleeding out. My fear escalated, and I began to vibrate myself, though nothing like my counterpart.

"Luke, the Thought Marker has presented itself. He is going to do it. I have an agreement, and I need you to sign it."

She sent me a document stating that we would be partners in a global campaign called Operation Stopgap. I was to be her Colonel. Her navigator, if you will, and she was the General in charge of formal executions. I read the document over three hundred times in a few seconds but couldn't yet bring myself to sign it. I had too many questions. There were too many implications associated with this kind of operation.

"What if your Thought Marker theory is wrong?"

"It's not, and Diana and her husband are going to find out the hard way."

Diana's husband, James, flicked on the light in the master bedroom and bolted out of bed. He called out, asking who was there. He threatened to call the police and picked up the phone. I connected with Diana, who knew exactly who was in the house, and why. Her heart redlining as she sat up in bed.

She had known as soon as the dog barked, although she couldn't believe it was actually happening. *How did he find me? How did he possibly find me?*

Fear had her firmly by the throat, and sounds wouldn't take shape. She wondered if she should reach for the baby in the nearby crib but was paralyzed. Perhaps if she had the baby in her arms they might both be hit by gunfire. Diana grabbed a throw pillow and hugged it tightly, awaiting Calvin Handler. He entered the room moments later, gun drawn.

"Put the phone down," he said to James. "I came here for one of you, but if you don't put the phone down, your kid's an orphan. Try me."

James put the phone down on the bed.

"We are moments away here, Luke. This is going to happen," said Safia.

Calvin told James to get on the floor. James refused and motioned to protect Diana, so Calvin put a bullet in his abdomen, and James went down hard, clawing at the ever-expanding wine stain on his white T-shirt. Diana's eyes filled but she made no sound. She sat there, frozen.

Calvin raised the gun to her. This was the moment he had been rehearsing in his head, coming to fruition. The weight of the moment landed on him, and he smiled. He said, "For such a smart girl, how could you be so fucking stupid, Diana?"

He was pleased with that line and thought it captured exactly how he was feeling at the moment. Much better than the options he'd come up with in the car.

Diana managed to cough out a plea for forgiveness. To spare her life and that of her husband.

"No, no, no. This is not my fault," said Calvin. "That's not fair. This is *your* fault. *You* did this to yourself. *You* walked away from the cash cow we built, and I warned you this would happen if you did."

Diana just shook her head and sobbed.

Safia hovered closer to her.

"Luke, Diana's blood is on your hands. I can stop this, but you have to partner with me." And she sent me the document with the signature portion magnified and glowing. Calvin raised the weapon and placed his finger on the trigger.

There was no more time for the debate surrounding implications and morals, evolution and laws. All of that was now boring rhetoric with lives hanging in the balance.

I signed the document and sent it back to Safia.

"Goodbye, Diana," said Calvin. "It's just business, sweetheart."

The room shook with Safia's rage for exactly two seconds. Calvin Handler stood with a perplexed look on his face, as if someone had stumped him with a difficult math equation or asked him to spell "onomatopoeia" front to back, then back to front.

Blood began to pour from his nose and run from his eyes and ears.

He promptly dropped to the floor and made a mess of the lovely silk rug. Diana covered her mouth, but no scream came out. James continued to moan and writhe on the floor.

"What just happened? Diana? Where is he? Are you all right? Jesus Christ! Answer me!" said James, and he went on like that for thirty-three seconds before Diana made a peep. She told James he was going to live.

"Someone up there is looking out for us, love," she said.

Safia sent me a thousand roses and a card that read, "Congrats! Way to save a life."

"Now, we get to work," she said.

Thus began Operation Stopgap.

9

After the salvation of Diana, Safia and I met at the peak of Mount Everest and hovered there. The scene was postcard-perfect, as if Mother Nature were staging a photo shoot for tourism. Not a cloud in the sky. *The calm before the storm*, I thought, and Safia sent me a check mark.

"It looks like we're doing this," I said.

"Thankfully, yes."

"I'd like to know why my involvement and service is required before you go on your self-justified killing spree."

"First, let me tell you about Operation Stopgap," she said. "The world has been able to operate as it has for far too long. Too often, those who harm or kill others walk away with little to no punishment to speak of, and to be clear, I do not consider time behind bars or life in prison to be justice. Clearly, then, the criminal justice system in place is not working, nor is it terrifying enough to deter a person from committing atrocities. The world needs something to close the gap between violent crime and punishment. Thus, I present to you our operation. Anyone caught in an attempt to commit a malicious act toward another human being with the clear intent to maim, murder, or cause severe bodily harm is considered guilty, as per the mandate of Operation Stopgap. Upon identification of the Thought Marker, that individual is to be executed before the act of violence can be committed. Luke, this is where you come in. I cannot be gathering information and ending lives at the same time. There is too much information to process. I need you to collect the data. I need you to chart the thought patterns of malicious intent and rank those individuals according to Thought Markers and the time horizon of the event taking place," she said, and she showed me exactly how to do that. "You send me the coordinates of Thought Markers, and I will be racing around the world, protecting the innocent. It's that simple."

"You don't think any of this is wrong?"

"No," she said, and then sent me the full definition for the word "conviction," having circled the appropriate meaning in context to her passion project.

"Got it."

"This will be an exciting time for the world. A state of panic is highly probable, fraught with confusion and questioning, but the message will spread, and it will become a safe world. All on account of our work."

"Good work as in the prevention of harm and murder through murder," I said.

"Good work as in the protection of the innocent through the complete removal of harm and murder," she said and sent me a clip of a wrestler pinning another wrestler. The larger, more heavily muscled wrestler doing the pinning had SAFIA written on his red Lycra briefs in white block letters. You can imagine whose name was written on the wrestler being pinned, the one in the blue briefs.

"I guess you have me there," I said and sent her back the laugh track from a nineties sitcom.

She sent me back a smile. A simple one, like you'd find in a children's sticker book.

"I have some serious concerns about the Bookkeeper," I said.

"Why? He's been nothing but silent."

"That's part of my concern. Why has he been so silent? We're moments away from dramatically altering what was meant to be."

"What if *this* was meant to be, Luke," she said and sent me a wink. I plowed through her mandate once again, looking for loopholes out of the mess I had gotten myself into.

"I think we should discuss the act of self-defence," I said. "There's no mention of it in here. "

"Good point. Acts of self-defence do not breed Thought Markers. In these cases, a fight or flight instinct entirely drives the decision-making process. So, when flight is taken out of the equation, leaving someone backed into a corner their instinct will be to fight. In fighting for their lives, the innocent may severely injure or murder the assailant coming at them; however, no Thought Marker is produced. It is all a wash of fear and survival driven by the desire to escape. Due to this, I left the act of self-defence from the mandate entirely. Besides, twenty-four or forty-eight hours from now, when the world understands that peace is demanded of it, the act of self-defence will not be required."

"This is really happening," I said and sent her a document through which she could opt out of the operation and terminate our contract.

Safia shared with me a digital clock counting down from ten seconds. "Yes, Luke. This is happening."

The clock reached zero.

"You're the Colonel, Luke. Please tell me where I am headed first."

The time had come to fulfill my end of the bargain. Any attempts to talk her out of this crazy plan had failed miserably, and worse, I had failed as a Mentor. More than just me, It seemed like the whole system had failed her, but who was I to question a system that had been in place long before Luke James Stevenson was crushed in an intersection and opted to come back as a ghost?

Diana was alive, and this was the price.

That was the deal.

Colonel Luke Stevenson at your service.

Just as she had taught me, I connected to the cumulative thought projections of the planet and then grouped, batched, and charted the projections as per malicious intent, conditions, context, and Thought Markers. Ninety-five Thought Markers were Code Red, which meant that those individuals had not only reached the point of no return as per committing the violent crimes, but that the crimes were likely to take place within the next sixty seconds or less. Of those Markers, I organized them in order of occurrence and sent to Safia the global coordinates.

She thanked me and left to do her work.

• • •

She reached eighty-nine of the ninety-five Code Red targets in time, a few with only a second or two to spare before crimes were committed. But there were six she didn't reach. I'll never forget those six for as long as I'm able to recall. The sour luck of those six, the fear they felt, the pain, all due to the time I had wasted arguing with Safia and looking for loopholes to get out of the deal.

Me.

I was responsible for those six.

Luke James Stevenson, the jeweller from Oakville, could have saved their lives. I felt the throes of remorse when that reality settled in. Those six souls weighed on me, and no amount of perspective was helping. If anything, after botching the data, I was hungry to save more lives. The entire mindset of the operation was twisting its way into making sense, and it scared me to think that I might start thinking like her.

Like Safia.

An apology letter was crafted, and I sent it off to Safia with respect to the unfortunate six. She sent me back a short clip of a boxer sitting in his corner after round one — eyes puffy and bleeding from both nostrils. The old coach screaming in his ear, "Get up, kid! You're just getting started!"

In sports, as in life, nothing motivates more than a good mentor and the sting of defeat. It was time to channel my energy, honour my commitment, and get back in back ring. Thought Marker after Thought Marker surfaced on the Code Red screening system, and precise coordinates were sent Safia's way. I'll say this much: In a short amount of time, we settled into a nice workflow as the body count rose.

10

The first several hundred executions were a breeze. Cut-and-dry cases. Situations in which I felt we were doing some good. Maybe even something heroic in nature. Innocents were being saved from certain death, danger, or dismemberment. However, within the first thousand executions, a few unique situations surfaced in the Conditions and Context portion of the screening system. In cases such as these, I would travel to the destination personally to assess the situation before calling in Safia to deal the death blow. The first unique situation required an amendment to be written, titled "Captive Cathy Anne."

Outside the city of Espanola, New Mexico, on Interstate 84, a trucker named Dale Henry had picked up a middle-aged woman named Cathy Anne Frank whose day, in a nutshell, had gone to hell. Her car died, but before her car died, her cellphone died. So Cathy Anne Frank, saddled with a dead car and dead phone, waved down an eighteen-wheeler and met its driver, Dale Henry.

Dale Henry pulled his rig to the side of the interstate.

Dale Henry offered her an energy drink because she was thirsty.

Dale Henry offered her a chocolate bar and half a bag of Doritos because she was hungry.

"Thanks so much for all of this help," said Cathy Anne. "You're such a nice guy. You never know who you're going to get when you're waving someone down. You know?"

"It's true," he said. "You're a lucky gal."

"I am, indeed. Thank God," she said.

When I found Cathy Anne Frank, she was tied to a chair in Dale Henry's shed with duct tape over her mouth. After serious consideration and a few conversations in his head with God, the two of them had come to the conclusion that the best thing for everyone involved in this predicament was to end the life of Cathy Anne and then have Dale dispose of the body as best he could. So far, Dale's top choice in the category of body disposal was to dig a big hole, bury her in it, and plant a tree overtop to make it look like he had just … planted a tree. He stood before Cathy Anne with his hands on his hips, wiping sweat from his brow every five seconds or so. He had originally thought of using a gun or blunt instrument, but when he and God chose to kill Cathy Anne, God demanded that the murder be carried out with bare hands. That having to physically strangle the life out of Cathy Anne would be punishment enough for Dale's lack of good judgment thus far. The strangulation of Cathy Anne was the only way Dale could purify himself and still get to Heaven. Dale, in fact, desperately wanted to go to Heaven. His mother was up there, and he missed her tremendously. God had told Dale that he and Dale's mother played bridge every Thursday evening and that she was always telling stories of Dale growing up.

And what a fine child he was. How proud of him she was.

Until now, that is.

God and Dale's mother were not impressed with this recent bout of indiscretion regarding Cathy Anne Frank. However, thankfully, salvation was only one strangulation away. Sadly, for Cathy Anne, Dale was committed to righting his wrong. Committed to God in Heaven and his mother. Committed to a seat at the Thursday evening hand of bridge at the big man's table, and he would do whatever it took to earn that seat.

Dale rolled up his camouflage sleeves while walking in circles around Cathy Anne's chair on the dirt floor of the shed. He cracked his knuckles a few times and repeated, "Here we go," over and over again. And, "This is for you, God. This is for you, Mama."

Cathy Anne knew this was the end.

Any shred of hope had now been extinguished. Part of her welcomed the end.

She wondered what her kids might grow up to be. She wondered when her husband might move on, and how long his grieving period might last. *Maybe a year*, she thought. That would be a fine amount of time, and then he could get out there again. She worried about whom he might select as a mate, given his chequered history of dating. She worried about who might end up tucking her son and daughter in at night, and if her children would eventually come around to accept the replacement. She wondered if they would ever call the replacement "Mom." That made Cathy Anne terribly sad. She wondered if anyone would find her body or bones at all, but thought it might be better if they didn't. The debate raged in her mind: Was it better to be found dead and allow her kids a sense of closure, or never to be found and have her kids believe she might be alive somewhere, having abandoned them? Cathy Anne, with no real power to control any outcome at this point, slammed a gavel on the judge's stand in her mind and ruled that being found dead would be best.

Closure would be best for the kids.

Dale's Thought Marker was into Code Red, but something didn't add up. A logical issue had presented itself that brought me to his shitty old shed outside of Espanola in the first place. I called Safia to the scene.

"Are we ready to go here?" she said.

"The Thought Marker is clear, but you can't execute this one," I said.

"Why not?"

"This woman is bound to a chair. If you kill Dale Henry, Cathy Anne dies of either thirst or starvation."

"Cathy Anne is going to die anyway. Dale's Thought Marker is clear."

"I understand that, however, does executing Dale make things better or worse for Cathy Anne?"

"Better."

"Better? How do you figure that?" I said.

"Dale is punished, and she gets to live."

"For how long does she get to live before she starves to death?"

"I don't know. That is not my concern, really. Either way, she dies."

"So death due to strangulation is better than death due to starvation? Are we actually ranking this now?"

"If I don't kill Dale Henry, she dies at the hand of her captor. If I kill Dale Henry, she witnesses a miracle and dies by a function of being human. So you tell me what is better."

This point of hers was a hell of a good one.

"I think we have to kill Dale Henry," I said. "But I've only come to that conclusion due to the off chance she could still be found alive."

"Then we have our answer, don't we?"

"We do. If the execution of the assailant could result in the death of the victim by means of exposure or starvation, the assailant is still to be terminated due to the fact that the fate of the victim was already set in stone via the Thought Marker."

"I don't think we need an amendment to the mandate for that," she said, and she was correct. But what if Dale Henry wasn't going to kill her? What if this was another sexual assault? What then? I posed this question, and Safia buzzed around the room.

"In that case, your mandate states that you must kill Dale," I said, "and Cathy Anne dies of starvation, despite the fact that the assailant had no intention of killing her."

"The assailant must die in that situation, having violated the mandate."

"But wait — the life of the victim isn't in question in this case. Their mental and physical well-being is certainly in question, and the crime is terrible, but their life is not in danger. What then?"

"This operation is about the termination of violent crimes. If a victim dies due to being held captive while a violent crime is about to take place ... then that victim will require more help than just me."

"Respectfully, I don't think that's good enough. If life is a gift, and this mandate is about protecting the innocent, I don't believe an innocent bound to a chair or otherwise can die as the result of the execution of an assailant when their life was never on the line to begin with."

Safia paused and shook the shed. Some tools fell off the wall. Dale took this as a sign from God to get things going. "You are annoying me," she said.

"That means I'm likely right on this one."

In the end, it was agreed that in cases of violent crimes involving a captive innocent where the assailant did not intend murder, the assailant would not be executed, so long as the captive innocent willed to live and was holding out for escape and survival. If the victim wished to die rather than endure what was imminent, then the assailant was to be executed, and it would be left to fate for the trapped or bound survivor. In furtherance to that, two more issues were agreed upon: should a captive be forced to devise a plan to kill or severely injure their captor as their only means of escape, they would not be held accountable for the acts of violence, even if the plan to injure or kill was premeditated and produced a Thought Marker; secondly, anyone attempting to kidnap or take hostage an individual against their will would be found guilty and face death.

"I think these are important additions to the mandate," she said.

"Thanks for talking it through."

"Thanks for being such a strong Colonel," she said and sent me a solid gold star hanging from a red-and-white ribbon.

Safia wrote the first amendment and its subsections to Operation Stopgap, and that amendment was called "Captive Cathy Anne." We both initialled it and focused our attention back on Dale Henry, who was now dangerously close to carrying out his deadly agreement with the Lord. Dale put his trembling hands around Cathy Anne's neck. He massaged the muscles in and around the area for several seconds, but the grip began to tighten and tighten.

Cathy Anne said a prayer.

And just like that, Dale collapsed to the floor, bleeding profusely from the nose, eyes, and the ears.

Cathy Anne heard the weight of Dale meet the ground and opened her eyes. She was lodged somewhere between confusion and joy. She cried and thanked God. This was strange, since she had previously thanked God for delivering Dale Henry to her in the first place while attempting to flag down a ride. I sent Safia the Alanis Morissette song "Ironic." She played it a few times, actually.

"Maybe someone will find her," said Safia, and sent me the image of a sterling silver bracelet. The bracelet was loaded with little pewter charms, all of which were in the shape of hearts with the word "hope" stamped into them.

"Maybe they will. Maybe they won't," I said. "But I know we did the right thing here.

• • •

The second amendment to the code was titled "Forced Hand." This situation presented itself just minutes before Safia's first mass execution. I had sent along the coordinates of a small village in the Democratic Republic of Congo. Just outside the village, military Jeeps approached, loaded with three dozen armed rebels. These rebels had a terrible habit of slaughtering entire villages, and the next small village on the kill list was unknowingly about to be wiped out. Orders from the top were clear: kill every man, woman, and child. Take the teenage boys as prisoners. The teenage boys, of course, would be trained, indoctrinated, and become rebel killing machines of the future.

The jeeps came to a halt at the village outskirts. Men and boys jumped down from their vehicles, machetes in hand and guns loaded. It had only been sixteen days since this same group of rebels had slaughtered a village just like this one, to the east by a few dozen miles. One of the rebels, a boy eighteen years of age, thought that he might not swing so forcefully with his machete this time around. Sixteen days ago, he had buried it in a small child's skull and spent a good five minutes trying to get it out. Another young rebel wondered if these villagers, unlike the last group, might put up less of a fight during the rapings. Sixteen days ago, his face had been badly clawed and a piece of flesh torn from his arm by the teeth of a young girl. This time around, he thought it best to knock them unconscious or heavily daze them before proceeding.

One of the rebels was a twenty-one-year-old boy named Bonyeme. Of the three dozen rebels, he had no intention of being there, nor did he want to kill anyone. What Bonyeme wanted was to go home to his parents. However, the rebel leaders had made it very clear that this was not an option. If you do not fight, we will kill you, and then we will kill your family. Those were the rules. Thus, Bonyeme's actions, even sixteen days ago when this group slaughtered ninety-one innocents, were not only for his own survival, but also for the survival of his own flesh and blood back home.

A local father on a walk with his two young girls saw the rebels jump down from their Jeeps and prepare for battle. The father protectively tucked his offspring behind his trembling legs and suggested that the rebels go away. He suggested that this village was a peaceful one and that no one wanted any trouble.

"Safia, we are moments away here. I need to discuss Bonyeme. Is he a killer, or are his actions merely out of survival and for the survival of his family?"

"If he attempts to murder, I am taking his life."

"Right, but you're not giving him a chance. His Thought Marker will reveal itself, because those who are forcing his hand are still alive beside him."

"Continue."

"In situations where orders to kill are given from a superior, forcing the hand of an individual fearing for their lives (or the lives of loved ones), should we not execute the individual who gives the orders first and allow those who have no interest in violence the option to lay down arms and walk away?"

"It's not quite there yet," she said. "Keep going."

"Look, I can see Thought Markers as well, but if you look closely at Bonyeme's Thought Marker, it seems to be underscored with the desire for peace; that under different circumstances, his Thought Marker would not exist. I suggest we continue to execute those without this underscore but allow those with it the opportunity to lay down weapons. My prediction is that once you remove the authoritative figure giving the orders for murder, the Thought Marker will disappear in Bonyeme's case, as will others who underscore their Marker with the wish for peace."

For a moment her vibrations were still.

"This amendment has further repercussions," she said.

"Such as ..."

"I want this updated across the board, not simply in this case. The ordering of killings or violent crimes from this moment forward are now punishable by death."

"If it saves the life of Bonyeme and those like him, I'm all for it."

"I love it, and it shall be written," she said and sent me a second gold star — this one larger than the last, and more decorative. A star within a star, and trimmed with diamonds. From what I could tell, VVS1, D-colour, excellent cut stones. Twenty-five points apiece. "Congratulations, Colonel."

I sent her back a formal appraisal on the gems.

The second amendment to the mandate, "Forced Hand," was written in seconds and we both initialled the pages.

The leader of the group, an older rebel with a keloid scar running northeast to southwest over one eye, walked toward the father of two. He paused briefly and drew the machete from his belt. He asked the father of two by which means he would prefer his daughters die, the gun or the blade.

The leader held both weapons out in plain sight for the man to see.

The father of two begged for the lives of his girls.

"Fine," the rebel said. "I'll choose," and raised the machete high.

Then blood ran from profusely from his face.

He coughed. Gurgled a bit. And collapsed.

The scene stood still. In fact, if an artist were to paint an iconic image of Operation Stopgap, it would have been that exact image. The moment right before the first rebel fell. When he was still gurgling on his own blood and the machete had fallen forty-five degrees in his limp hand. The moment when his right knee had begun to buckle due to his dead weight. And the crying father of two left frozen with his hand in the air looking to protect his girls with bare flesh and bone.

That exact moment.

That was Safia's Operation Stopgap to a T.

The father looked up, speechless. He wanted to pray out loud but couldn't make his mouth work. Couldn't make anything work, really. He just sat up making a sound like he was choking or was parched for water.

The second-in-command stepped forward and promptly fired bullets into the air. He followed the gunshots with a battle cry — the signal for the men to commence their own mandate of ending lives. A starter's pistol, if you will, and off they ran, like screaming banshees, fuelled by a false sense of duty and the thrill of it all. Bonyeme wondered what he had just witnessed. He wondered if someone was listening to his prayers, and if this was a sign for him to sneak away. He wondered how many people he would have to kill before he could simply disappear without anyone noticing, never to have to kill again. The herd continued to charge ahead, machine guns and machetes drawn.

Villagers heard the shots and battle cry.

Mothers grabbed children.

Husbands grabbed wives.

Brothers grabbed sisters.

People grabbed people.

That same lone father, the one who had protected his two girls in the dirt, got the sense that someone was listening. That someone or something was protecting the village. On trembling legs, he slowly made his way to standing and extended an open hand — demanding that the charging rebels stop in their tracks.

Then came a series of heavy thuds, like the sky had opened up and rained bricks on the dry earth.

Then nothing.

Just the sounds of birds and wind.

That father of two, he just stood staring at the second miracle before him.

There lay thirty-five dead rebels. And there stood Bonyeme, machine gun in hand — frozen.

The villagers peeked out of their hiding places. White-knuckled grips on the garments of loved ones relaxed, and one by one, curious faces started to poke out, asking why their lives had been spared. Asking what had happened. Soon the entire village was standing before the dead rebels, all bleeding from the eyes, nose, and ears. All that blood feeding the thirsty cracks in the earth. The entire village gathered around the father, staring at Bonyeme.

"It was you," said the father. "Why did you do it? Why did you kill all of your friends?"

"It was not me," said Bonyeme.

"What is your name?"

"My name is Bonyeme. But I did not save you. This was not by the hand of man. This was something else. God, maybe."

"Do you plan to kill us now?"

"No," said Bonyeme. "No, I do not want to kill anybody. I just want to go home. I just want to see my family."

"Why did God spare you?" asked the father of two.

"I believe he heard my prayers and saw the true nature of my heart. I believe he chose to me spread the word, which I intend to do if you will let me go peacefully."

The villagers agreed.

Bonyeme dropped the machine gun, climbed into one of the Jeeps, and drove off in a cloud of dust.

The locals conversed and then began to pray. Two things were clear in their estimation: that father of two was a hero, and Bonyeme was the son of God.

• • •

Safia's form was swollen with pride. She vibrated with such happiness that the locals thought God was talking back to them, as if to say, "You're welcome."

"I *am* saying you're welcome to them. They just don't know it's me."

"Does that make you God?"

"Maybe it does," she said.

In the Post-Death Line, I had lived the life of the top Elvis impersonator in Las Vegas. The physical resemblance and performance similarity was nothing short of astounding. I sent her a clip of "Don't Be Cruel" from one of my sold-out shows at the Luxor Hotel.

"Or maybe you're just putting on one hell of a show," I said.

"Maybe I am. But I'll tell you this: I've never been so happy. Not in my life or in any of the lives I lived in the Line. This is the pinnacle of my existence, and because of that, I do feel godly."

"Old Testament God, maybe. The angry one." Well, she found that hilarious. She sent me back a clip of a wispy-haired, obese American man literally laughing himself to death after telling a joke at a dinner party. The man was wearing a plastic lobster bib that read "Frank Family Lobsterfest." I'll admit, his laughter at the beginning was truly hilarious. However, the end of the clip was terribly dark. This was Safia, after all. Not exactly equal parts light and dark.

"I didn't think my line was that funny," I said. "It was a bit passive-aggressive."

"Firstly, do not ever compare what I'm doing to any form of organized religion. Secondly, if we are not playing God, we are playing hero, and I am fine to wear that title."

"Are we playing hero?"

"If this were a novel, wouldn't I be the hero?" she said, and sent me all of the epic novels I had ever read where the hero saves the innocent via the slaying of villains and monsters.

"That's me, Luke," she said. "I am the slayer of monsters. I thought you loved those stories?"

"I do love those stories."

"Then this should be a dream come true, because you are slaying monsters with me!" she said. I sent her a video clip of my grandfather telling me to be careful what you wish for.

By that time new Thought Markers of soon-to-be criminal behavior had reached Code Red status, and I had new execution coordinates for Safia.

She sent me a clip of a pit bull licking its chops.

Then she left.

• • •

Within the first thousand executions, two more situations were presented that required no amendment to the mandate but provided cause for pause. Southeast of Moscow, where the Moskva and Oka rivers converge, rests the city of Kolomna. A Thought Marker called me to an apartment building in this ancient meeting place, where I hovered over a woman named Malvina Pravdin. Malvina was kneeling by the side of the tub as her six-year-old daughter, Yana, played with a plastic boat and rubber animals. Yana was attempting to pack as many animals on the boat as possible, but the boat always tipped over. Not all could fit. Yana's biggest issue was choosing which animals would make it onto the boat.

Malvina's biggest issue was that Carla had taken over her brain and was in control of her bodily functions. Moreover, Carla was only moments away from drowning Malvina's daughter, Yana. You see, Carla was nothing but resentful of Yana. Little Yana was held responsible for many things. For ruining Carla's first and second marriages. For ruining her flat tummy and for the scar on it where the doctors cut her open and made a Russian doll out of her. She blamed little Yana for the stretch marks on her breasts and the matching set on her hips. For the emergence of the kinked and wiry grey hairs that now populated her once gorgeous head of hair. For the wrinkles in her forehead and the bags under her eyes. For killing her free time and ability to find another man.

That's the way she saw it, anyway.

Yana: the cancer. A cancer that needed removal.

In turn, Malvina despised Carla, and passionately so. But Carla was far stronger than Malvina, and when she took over, Malvina ran like a scared little girl and cowered in the recesses of her own mind. She found a dark corner in a fold of brain, went fetal, and shivered. Sometimes, when Carla was in control, she would leave Yana in the house and go out drinking. Sometimes Carla would return with a man, and Malvina would be left to clean up the mess the next morning and suffer the hangover. Sometimes

Carla would leave work early, claiming to be sick, score pills or powder, and forget to pick up Yana from school. Malvina would be the one to explain what happened to the teachers and school administration. Carla would forget to cook dinner, and Yana would go hungry those nights. Carla wouldn't cook breakfast or pack a lunch for Yana, and Yana wouldn't learn much at school those days. Carla would puke all over the bathroom or kitchen, and Malvina would clean it up.

Malvina was a professional Carla cleaner-upper.

Sadly, on this particular evening, Carla was determined to remove the cancer from her life. Cancer that was deep in the process of loading rubber animals on a plastic boat that invariably dumped over time and time again.

Carla had decided to get into the tub and pin the little girl underwater. Strangling leaves marks, and she needed to do her best to make it look like an accidental drowning. After Yana was gone, Carla planned to get a frying pan and give little Yana a ding on the back of the head to make it seem as though she had slipped in the tub, lights-out, and the rest you already know.

Meanwhile, Malvina was watching these plans take shape from that tiny recess, that dark fold in the brain. Chained there. Wailing in agony for Carla to stop.

Two thought projections — one brain.

Two distinct people — one body.

I called Safia, and she arrived, promptly.

I asked how she was doing, and she sent me the image of a Samurai warrior covered in the hot, dripping red of battle.

Fair enough.

"We may have an issue here," I said and uploaded to her the situation at hand.

"I see no issue," she said.

"We haven't discussed the mentally ill," I said. "These people are sick. Malvina here is sick. She needs help."

"I see a clear Thought Marker, Luke. That woman is about to drown that little girl. Might I suggest that the little girl needs help?"

"It's Carla's Thought Marker. Not Malvina's."

"This is not a rehabilitation program, Luke. We are in the business of protecting the innocent. Malvina may be ill, yes. However, her daughter is about to be murdered if we do nothing."

"By Carla's hand."

"By a hand that shares their mutual DNA. While I agree that this isn't necessarily Malvina's fault, there is a clear Thought Marker, and a life will be saved. The cost of that is a life taken. This will always be the case, regardless of mental illness or not. Are we clear on this issue?"

"It still seems grey."

"Put differently, I ask you this: Who would you prefer dies in this situation? Because someone has to die in order for the other to live."

"Yana can't die."

"I am in agreement, and we have our answer for this particular case, and all cases like it going forward."

"I suppose we do."

"I see no reason to update the mandate. Do you?

"I don't. No," I said.

Carla stood and looked down at Yana in the tub. The crime was moments away. Carla smiled at Yana, and Malvina screamed for Yana to run, but sound doesn't travel well from the recesses of the mind. Yana saw the smile on her mother's face.

She smiled back and mentioned how much she loved to see her mother smile. The smile didn't last long. Safia did her thing, and that smile drooped, and Malvina and Carla's shared face bled from the eyes, ears, and nose. They both free-fell to the floor, where Malvina's head cracked open, and out spilled Carla onto the tile and grout.

Yana screamed.

The rubber animals sank to the bottom of their ocean, and the plastic boat bobbed up and down in the storm of waves. Sure, the child was scarred for life, but she was alive. I felt as though we had done a good thing there. Safia sent me a clip of a pat on the back. I sent her the image of a bottle of vodka and a wedding-style invitation card with the suggestion that we share it.

"The only think I get drunk on is saving lives," she said, and off she went.

• • •

Another unique situation was the case of the jumper at the Millau Viaduct in France — the tallest vehicular bridge in the world. When I found Lucien Leroy, he had long since pulled his car over and sat balancing on the long horizontal guardrail looking down into the valley. His mind was an electrical storm of images and sound bites, video clips, and newspaper articles surrounding the major collision he had been involved in.

The one in which he had become infamous.

The one where he'd been blind drunk, staggered from the bar to his car, and then wiped out two teenagers coming home from a movie. The movie they were coming home from was about a drunk driver who copes with wiping out two teenagers coming home from a movie.

Frozen inside Lucien's mind was the front page of a French newspaper that roughly translated to: *Tragedy Marries Irony*. Then flashed an Internet article that read: *Lucien or Lucifer? It Is for You to Decide*. The cartoon artist in this case had certainly given her all with respect to the featured caricature. Tail and horns. Cloven hoof. The whole nine yards. It was a terrific work of art. Then a newscast showing Lucien's face as the anchor spoke about the tragic accident. Then another.

Then another.

Then another.

Lucien sat there balancing on the guardrail. He imagined his lapse in judgment would define him for the rest of his life. He imagined running away to Thailand and checking into a disgusting Bangkok hotel. The kind where rats board for free. The kind where insects might feed on feces or something that was once human and was forgotten about. He imagined the front desk clerk looking at his identification and pointing his index finger. "It's you. You're the drunk monster who killed those two kids coming home from a movie about a drunk monster who kills two kids coming home from a movie. Isn't it! It's you!" And then he called more people over to point fingers at him.

Lucien imagined confronting his mother in the nursing home and what she might say to him. The look in her eyes. The realization that her own life would now be solely defined as the mother whose son was the drunk monster. He imagined her writing a memoir: *Mother of the Most Hated Man in France for a Period in Time*. How could he stand before her? Her pointing finger was longer than any other in the world. It had the ability to breach Lucien's ribcage and skewer his heart.

No, Lucien couldn't see his mother ever again.

That was for sure.

He couldn't watch the news or read the paper or surf the Internet ever again.

He couldn't enjoy a cup of coffee or a glass of wine ever again. Why should he? Why should he get to enjoy anything ever again? *Those two young teens coming home from a movie can't enjoy anything,* he thought.

His Thought Marker was clear. He was surely about to kill.

But kill himself.

I called Safia. "What do we do here?" I said.

"What would you like to do?"

"Stop him."

"How? By killing him?"

"I was called here because of his Thought Marker. Are we to kill people before they kill themselves?"

"No," she said. "They are hurting themselves, not others."

"In hurting themselves, they will surely hurt others."

"This mandate deals with physical hurt or death, not emotional hurt or emotional death. I can't fix everything, Luke."

And that was that.

Lucien slid off the guardrail and felt the surge of adrenaline. The kind of rush you might get on the down slope of the world's tallest roller coaster or skydiving. He flew for a few seconds, and in those seconds he was no longer the drunk driver or the lead story on a newscast. He wasn't the inspiration for memes or mean comments on Internet news pages or posts on social media. At that moment in time, he was just something falling quickly from one place to another, affected by nothing but gravity.

"What about his act of drunk driving?" I said. "He did kill those kids. Are drunk drivers to be added to the list as well?"

"Are those travelling above the speed limit to be executed, Luke?"

"No, I said. That's too far."

"There is nothing I can do about accidents. They happen too quickly and without a Thought Marker. It is all but impossible to track the offenders."

"I'm sure we could design something," I said.

"Look at you," she said, and sent me a smile. "It seems as though you are thinking of new ways to remove dangerous people from the world?"

"I don't know what I'm thinking. I'm just looking for gaps in logic."

"If the drunk driver gets into his car and has clear intent to kill someone, we terminate that person. If the highway speeder has the undeniable intention to lose control and wipe people out, we terminate that person. If Thought Markers aren't present, I'm not interested with interfering. We have to focus on intentional acts of violence. But I applaud your thinking on the matter."

"I'm not finished discussing this one," I said.

"Neither am I. Let's discuss this again once all the rubbish has been bagged."

Then she left.

11

Within the first forty-eight hours, Safia had executed 177,551 people. As predicted, news of the miraculous events spread like wildfire around the globe. Networks and newspapers became inundated with calls and emails. The Internet exploded via social media and chatrooms. Reporters and journalists raced around interviewing survivors after would-be victims of violent crime — all sharing similar tales of salvation in the face of certain death or serious personal injury. Many seemed stuck between shock and disbelief. Many were overcome with emotion, bordering on unintelligible, doing their best to force out the story between sobs and the stuttered sucking in of air. Eyes were wiped with hands and nostrils with sleeves, thankful that someone or something was listening to their cries for help.

That someone or something had cared enough to intervene.

Of course, that someone or something was typically God.

That was, unless the praise was saviour-specific. In that case, all credit was given to one of the four usual suspects.

It was God in all but a small handful of cases where aliens were thought to be responsible. Staunch atheists, even in the face of such miraculous salvation, were still on the fence as to what exactly had taken place, not yet willing to admit it was by the hand of an omnipotent creator. Largely, they remained in the camp they hung out in the most.

The "I don't know" camp.

The "not enough evidence" camp.

The "I believe nothing of what I hear and only half of what I see" camp.

The atheists were aware that something important was going on and that someone or something was interfering. But damned if they were lining up to have their heads dunked in holy water any time soon.

"What we've all seen doesn't prove the existence of God by any means," one atheist said to a reporter. "Someone could appear and turn all of my tap water into draught beer, and I'd still be asking some hard questions."

Without question, this forty-eight-hour period was a terribly exciting time on Earth. One could argue it was the most exciting time in the history of humankind. Images of deceased assailants bleeding from the eyes, nose, and ears raced around news outlets and social media, all with personal and eyewitness accounts of the miraculous events. And as much as I was still sitting on the moral fence as to what Safia and I were doing, it was impossible for me to deny the level of excitement we had caused. And not just for the living. Safia wondered if we had programmed the greatest entertainment for ghosts in the history of ghosting. Hard to disagree, I supposed.

Families from all over the world huddled around twenty-four-hour news channels listening to anchors and reporters, professors, religious leaders, and military elite all doing their best to make sense of what was going on.

The BBC organized a panel of the world's top political scientists to weigh in on the governmental repercussions facing several countries around the world that were currently without their leaders.

Those leaders had been found in their offices bleeding from the eyes, ears, and nose or had dropped dead in front of their advisors. One even died during a press conference. Those leaders, of course, had given approval for their military commanders to carry out war crimes and thus violated the Forced Hand amendment.

"What is to become of these leaderless countries?" asked the mediator.

"A large part of me is quite certain that the countries we are discussing here today, which are now thankfully without their leaders, are far better off going forward," said a poli-sci professor from Harvard, using aggressive air quotations on the *leaders* part.

"If this trend of miraculous intervention continues," said a poli-sci professor from Oxford, "the days of dictatorships and despotism are over. As far as politics is concerned, the use of threats and fear to shape countries has gone the way of the dodo. People shouldn't be hiding under their beds — they should be out in the streets celebrating! By and large, the people of the world are finally free."

Top medical professionals around the globe began to weigh in on the physical nature of the deaths. Many suggested that it could be some form of global disease or virus but couldn't explain why death occurred at the precise moment when acts of violence were about to occur. CNN brought in a panel of experts to discuss that possibility.

"Perhaps the disease or virus turns deadly upon the highest levels of endorphin or serotonin release, as would be the case when committing crimes of this nature," said a professor of medicine at NYU.

"Beats me," said a professor of medicine at McGill University. "If that were the case, we'd all be dropping dead of coitus."

Al Jazeera brought top religious leaders from around the world together in a round table to discuss why people of all faiths and people of no faith were being saved from the acts of violence. Did this suggest there was only one God? What did that mean for the major world religions? Had their dogma been debunked?

One religious leader suggested that it was all of the Gods working together, just like all of the people on Earth needed to work together to create peace and sustainability.

This hypothesis was largely shot down due to unpopularity.

Another religious leader, wearing a massive cross around his neck, suggested that there was only one God, and that this was most likely the second coming of Christ.

"This is just the tip of the iceberg," he said. "The worst is yet to come. Praise Jesus. That's what we should all be doing," he said. Others on the panel listening to this scratched their heads and beards. Others shook their heads in disbelief.

A young religious leader wearing a yarmulke said, "I think that whether we want to admit it or not, a God who protects all people of all faiths turns current religious thinking on its ear. Perhaps it's time to throw out all of the old books and old thinking and go back to the golden rule."

"The future will certainly be interesting," said another leader in golden robes. "But one thing is for sure: whoever it is or whatever it is clearly upset with how we treat one another. And I can't blame them."

That last comment went viral.

Safia even made a habit of sending me that particular sound bite whenever she carried out an execution. She would follow the sound bite with a video clip of a hammer hitting a nail on the head.

After a three full days, acts of violence had slowed down significantly as the world put two and two together. The warnings had successfully spread.

The message was clear.

Thus, my full attention wasn't required to track Thought Marker charts. The frequency had slowed so significantly that prioritizing executions wasn't difficult in the slightest. A Marker would present itself, and then I would promptly send the coordinates to Safia and return to what I was doing or go back to whoever I was watching/

hovering over. Typically, it was these panels of experts or in news-rooms around the world.

When the president of the United States was moments from speaking, I was hovering over Diana. She was in a hospital room, breastfeeding her baby, as she watched the debates and breaking news. Her husband, James, lay sleeping, covered in fresh white sheets, recovering from his surgery. Thankfully, he had survived the shooting, which thrilled me to no end. This was for three reasons: firstly, I would not be responsible for his death due to my late sign-ing of the Operation Stopgap mandate; secondly, Diana wouldn't be without the man she loved, and thirdly, their child would have the respectable father he deserved.

A nurse came in and asked Diana if she would like to watch the president's address to the nation on a bigger television.

"I've wheeled one of the big screens out from the rehab area for everyone in this wing to watch it," she said. Diana thanked her but admitted she would rather watch it on the small TV in the room and remain by her husband's side.

"Suit yourself," said the nurse.

As for me, I could have witnessed this presidential address from anywhere in the world. I could have been in the Oval Office, hov-ering above his shoulder, if I so chose. But what I chose was being with Diana.

Safia showed up, fresh from recent executions, and hovered beside me. "Seems to be a lull for the moment," she said.

"People are pretty confused right now."

"Did you think I would watch this historic address without you, My Colonel? My right-hand ghost? There's nowhere I'd rather be than watching this with you."

"I'm glad you're here, Safia. Thanks for joining," I said, but she read my thoughts and saw how much I had enjoyed being here alone with Diana.

"Is that true? I can leave if you are having a moment."

"It was just a passing thought. I'm glad you're here," I said and sent her the definition of "honesty."

She sent me a smile, and we hovered close together.

Diana, cradling the baby, got up from her chair and went over to James. She thought he had ripe armpits and needed a bath. She wondered when the nurses would come by to get that done and how qualified those nurses truly were. Why did James have to get the skinny little tarts fresh out of university? Why did they have attitude? They weren't digging ditches in the heat. They weren't working in a coal mine or raising condo towers in Dubai. They trained and signed up for this. To be nurses.

And Diana wanted only the best of nurses for James. She wanted the Michael Jordan of nurses, and then she imaged Michael Jordan in scrubs with white Birkenstocks. Specifically, the style that covers the toes. She imagined Nurse Jordan giving James a sponge bath while telling him behind-the-scenes details of the National Basketball Association. And then Diana laughed at herself while she softly stroked James's cheek with her index finger. She organized his mess of hair back to into something that resembled a natural part and thought how handsome he was.

"James, sweetie, the president of the United States is about to speak," she said.

James moved slightly but remained fast asleep. Diana thought it best not to wake him. She pressed down the edge of medical tape over his IV connection that had started to turn up, and then gently began to rock the baby.

This is what the president of the United States of America said to his fellow Americans, and to the world.

12

Good evening. For half a century now, the United States of America has undertaken the global responsibility to protect those who could not protect themselves. With strength of leadership, the might of our military, and the bravery of the men and women who populate our armed forces, America has risen time and time again to combat evil. For that, America has paid the ultimate price, with the lives of our heroic soldiers. Yet despite our best efforts, the lives of many innocent men, women, and children could not be saved. In my presidency and for those presidents before me, this has certainly been a source of frustration with respect to our military and peacekeeping efforts. Whether that means entering a conflict which has already claimed the lives of thousands or hundreds of thousands, or whether that means being present in battle and still unable to save every single innocent life — this weighs heavily on presidents, as it does America. However, we accept that this is the nature of war. That, despite our best efforts, the blood of innocents will be spilled by the hand of the enemy, and that it is our goal to save as many lives as we can. To free those who wish to be free.

To remove the enemy. To force their submission, and see that they do not rise again.

Nonetheless, American forces cannot be anywhere, any time, to save those in need. The global events of the last seventy-two hours may speak to the presence of another force.

A force we are unfamiliar with and a force we have yet to identify. Yet a force that seems to share with us the strong desire to protect the innocent.

A force that, from what we understand, seems to be anywhere and everywhere to intercept acts of violence and to ensure that no innocent is left behind.

A force that follows a rigorous moral code and a swift process for punishment. A process for punishment, I should say, that we are working around the clock to understand in greater detail.

What we know so far is that this process does not include our formalities of arrest, information-gathering, trial, and conviction. This process may not include what we consider as due process here in America, but I can assure you, this process does involve judgment, conviction, and serves the highest of penalties — death. From the intelligence we have gathered, we understand this much at present: any individual, regardless of country or creed, caught in the act of committing an act of violence toward their fellow man is likely to suffer death. At this time, we remain diligent in our efforts to collect more data.

I ask all of you today, as America asks of you each and every day, to be kind to your fellow man and to refrain from participating in any act that would cause bodily harm to another individual. In the past, failure to abide by this warning meant facing our own criminal code. It meant facing a judge or a jury. It meant sentencing based on the degree of crimes committed. It meant prison. It could mean psychiatric rehabilitation. And hopefully an eventual release back into society as a contributing citizen of America.

In most cases, it meant second chances.

Today, there are no second chances.

Today, failure to abide by this warning is most certainly at your peril.

Confusion and fear has befallen America, as it has the rest of the world. As intelligent beings, we seek answers. We seek to solve the most challenging equations and mysteries alike. We seek responsibility for actions. Therefore, we seek to understand who or what is responsible for the events of the last seventy-two hours. We seek to understand the full intentions of this force and whether we are dealing with a friend or an enemy.

Are these the actions of God?

Are these the actions of an alien race?

At present, we have nothing to report to the American public as to who may be responsible. If these acts are, indeed, by the hand of God, then our fate rests in his hands. If that is the case, our faith, the purity of our hearts, and our actions, both past and present, may dictate our future. If the thousands of reported killings are by the hand of an alien being or race, we will continue to do our best to communicate with those responsible and to further understand their policies and actions. If these acts are by the hand of an individual, terrorist group, or government, through the use of an advanced technology, you can be assured that we will get to the bottom of it.

Whether by the hand of God, alien race, or terrorist group, today we are being held to the highest accountability for our actions. Today it has been demanded of us to use the power of our minds when solving problems and not the force of our fists or the ease of our weapons. Today we have been asked to treat others as we would have them treat our mothers, fathers, sisters, brothers, aunts, uncles, friends, and ultimately, ourselves.

Today, peace has been demanded of us.

Knowing that many of you are in fear as to what will come next, let me suggest that perhaps we have less reason to be fearful than ever. If whoever is responsible for these actions can hear me now, let them hear me say this: for the thousands of families around the world who, because of your actions, get to hold their loved ones close tonight, I thank you. For your ability to protect the innocent where America and the peacekeeping countries around the world could not, I thank you again. As the president of the United States, and as a citizen of mankind, I would ask that you attempt to communicate with us to further our understanding of your motives and laws.

In the face of change, the functions of our government and our markets will remain operational. Life will go on. We will continue to conduct business and go about our lives. And as it seems, for now we may be able go about our lives more safely and happily than ever before.

God bless America.

13

I asked Safia for her take on the presidential address, and she sent me the image of a Do Not Disturb sign, a calculator, and a brain. So I did just that — I left her alone while she figured out her thoughts. Diana, now quite frustrated, repeatedly pressed the emergency button in hopes that a nurse might come to give James a bath. She debated pulling the fire alarm just to set off the sprinkler system. *At least that would provide him with a shower*, she thought.

Safia vibrated, and it shook the hospital room. The tongue depressors rattled together in their glass housing.

"This is fascinating," she said.

"What's that?"

"I pulled the thought projections from everyone who just watched that presidential address."

"And ..."

"Thirty-five percent thought he was sincere and telling the truth. Sixty-five percent thought he was lying and knew more than he let on. Seventy percent thought the events were by the hand of God, and I can show you the breakdown with respect to specific faiths if you want. Of the Christian group, forty-one percent saw it as the

Second Coming of Christ. That is to be expected. But this is really something: twenty percent of total viewers chalked the events up to aliens, and of that group, two percent thought the president to be an alien himself."

"Really?" I said.

"Yes."

"What are we supposed to do with that data?"

"Not much, but it did surface something that shocked me," she said, forwarding me the results page. "Not a single person thought that it might be the work of a ghost."

14

After a month, Operation Stopgap had slowed acts of violence to nothing. Absolutely nothing.

Zero. Zero violent crimes in the world.

As the president had suggested in his now-famous address, the world entered what many were calling the Age of Peace. Behavioural shifts were taking place. People were doing things they would never have done a month ago. They walked and jogged through parks at night, without a friend or can of mace for protection. People took to back alleys as shortcuts or went down formerly suspicious streets. In every dangerous slum, ghetto, and neighbourhood around the world, guns and knives were left at home. Rival gangs met and shook hands. People spoke their minds to partners, family members, and strangers, without the fear of physical harm or death for doing so. Women in suppressive or violent marriages walked out the front door, eager to start new lives. People married whom they wished. Parents stopped dropping their kids off at school if they were old enough to walk there and back.

Parks and playgrounds saw children playing unsupervised. Hitchhiking came back into fashion. People had begun to carry on conversations in subways, on trains and buses, and in the streets with complete strangers.

People were happy.

People were friendly.

People were more eager to help a stranger without the fear of being dismembered in their basement.

Religious debate was at an all-time high, but disagreements and heated arguments led to nothing more than continued discourse and sharper rhetoric. Without the threat of violence, the art of debate had improved globally. Logic, intellect, and the proper crafting of an argument became the new weapons of choice.

The only weapons of choice.

What good were fighter jets but for air shows? What good were tanks but for parades? What good were M16s, grenades, and missiles but for museums?

Scrap metal.

The entire war machine was nothing more than that, and shares of weapons manufacturers plummeted worldwide.

"We're not panicking yet," said the CEO of America's largest weapons manufacturer. "No one can be sure how long this divine intervention will protect the people of the world, and when things return to normal, we will hire back the hard-working citizens we have been forced to lay off. Full production will commence once again."

"Do you really believe that day will come?" asked the network interviewer.

"We certainly hope so."

"I just want to be clear," she said. "You *certainly hope* that the protection lifts and people can go back to killing each other with your weapons?"

The CEO was left with his mouth hanging open while the little mouse on the wheel in his mind worked overtime to come up with something appropriate to say. All the while it looked as though the well-groomed CEO might suffer a stroke or some sort of palsy.

Eventually, his mouth closed and he began spinning his wedding ring around his ring finger.

One.

Two.

Three.

Four.

Five times around went the ring.

Finally, this is what he came up with:

"Thanks for having me on today, Samantha. You're a real pleasure."

And the whole segment went viral.

• • •

Safia called me, and we met on the granite forehead of George Washington at Mount Rushmore. There she offered me a leave from my duties.

"That is until your services are required in the future," she said. "Then I will come calling."

"I hope you come calling before that," I said. "It gets lonely with no one to talk to."

"We did a great thing, Luke."

"I hope so."

"Look at the world," she said. "People are finally living."

"The world is certainly a different place."

"It's a better place," she said.

"Time will tell, I suppose."

"What do you mean by that?" she said and sent over a requisition for further explanation.

"You may have changed people's actions, but you haven't really changed people," I said. "Violent crimes have ceased because the punishment is both severe and unavoidable."

"Your point?"

"My point is that you've created a better system of policing. That's it. Yes, people have stopped harming one another, but it's simply because they can't get away with it. Humanity hasn't changed. Not from within. Not as it was intended, through experience and understanding over time. When your spirit lease is up, what then, Safia? Who's the police force then? After you're gone, how long until an individual has a knee-jerk, animal reaction to a situation and harms or kills someone? What then? News would spread like wildfire that the divine intervention, that the miraculous protection and the Age of Peace was over. Play that through for a second. What happens next? Does the world devolve back to a state of violent crime?" I said and sent her the definition of a rhetorical question. She crumpled the definition and sent it back on fire.

"Why would anyone lose sight of the punishment?"

"Because they are mammals! They are mammals armed with abstract thought and the ability to make decisions, but they are mammals, and mammals can be unpredictable. Mammals can get sick. What about those with mental illness? That's not going away any time soon, if ever. You'll be in What's Next, and some mentally ill person will get it in their head that they are communication with God and will be protected when they go on a killing spree. What happens when you are gone and that killing spree actually takes place?"

"It won't happen," she said.

I sent her a worn T-shirt with "Wishful Thinking" written in calligraphy. Behind the words were a gorgeous beach and sunset and a sign hanging from a palm tree that read, "Monday Morning." On the arm of a reclining beach chair rested a margarita.

"I have done good work! I have saved lives! The world is a better place!" she said.

I sent her a picture of the world with a Band-Aid wrapped around it. But the Band-Aid was soaking through, and a giant drop of blood was about to drop into space.

"That's all you've done, Safia," I said. "And just like Band-Aids invariably do, the corners are going to lose their stick. Then lift a little. Then it's just a matter of time before the whole thing flakes off." Before this, I had never seen Safia struggle so vigorously with a point of logic. Reviewing the history of all conversations with her, she had always produced a solid counter-argument, on average, within three Earth seconds. I sent her this data along with a running chronograph that was now at thirty-seven seconds.

She sent me back that Do Not Disturb sign.

I sent her back the video clip of an anaconda battling a giant crocodile. This was a popular video when I was alive on Earth. It had something like twenty million views. Except I tweaked it so that "My Point" was embossed on the anaconda, and "Safia" was embossed on the struggling crocodile.

She vibrated tremendously — one of the really scary category-two earthquake kind she could do so well.

Then she left.

15

After the argument with Safia, I checked in on my mother, who was gardening at the time. She thought she might purchase designer sunglasses like her fashionable neighbour Sue Dillon had from that discount website. She debated where to plant the sunflowers that she had purchased from the local garden centre and spent two hours picking the right spot. When trowel hit soil, the decision had been reached, given the variables of overall garden esthetics and total hours of sun exposure. That was her task for the day, and she had accomplished it. Post-planting, she sat in the tickle of freshly cut grass and moved her toes among the blades. She thought that she might go ahead with the bunion surgery after all and imagined herself crossing the line in next year's Oakville 5k Race to Cure Breast Cancer. Five kilometres of running, with no sections of walking, and raising a thousand dollars for every kilometre run. All of it in memory of her friend Betty Levinson, who had died a week ago. This was her new goal. She said a prayer to Betty and apologized for not attending the funeral. She hoped Betty would understand that she'd been to too many funerals lately and just wanted to garden and keep her thoughts clean and hands dirty. Then she swore at

Betty for not returning her sewing machine, and how the hell was she going to get that damn thing back now?

Mom was doing just fine.

I checked in on Diana, who was helping James into a steaming bath she had drawn for him. She wondered if she would ever get sick of drawing him a bath and concluded she wouldn't. After being gifted a longer life, she thought she could spend all day and night looking after her husband and child if need be, certain that she'd never be bored again. Ever. Diana squeezed the sponge over James's head and forgot whether or not the babysitter she had booked for next week had her first aid and CPR certifications. She made a mental note to ask. She considered getting back into the classroom sooner rather than later, since she desperately missed her students. She weighed the cost of daycare and decided it was worth it. Once James was healthy and back to work, she would get back to living her dream.

Diana was doing just fine.

I checked in on my sister Brooke and her husband Taitt — the poor guy who had suffered that horrendous nervous breakdown at my funeral. Taitt had left the investment business completely and was at home, working away on his animated children's book, *Snee the Sea Snake*. He fantasized about how many thousands of copies he might sell but concluded that reading the finished product to his forthcoming child would be reward enough. He wondered when he might read the story aloud to Brooke, since it was only moments away from being completed. No time was as good as the present, so he lit a fire, made a pot of mint tea, and asked Brooke to snuggle up with him on the couch.

There he pulled out the six pages of manuscript, stapled in the top left corner, and began to read aloud.

Brooke and Taitt were doing just fine.

I dropped in on Alice, who was now living with my best friend, Geoff Black. They sat together at the dinner table. Geoff thought her lasagna was a science experiment gone wrong. Something that might come to life in his gut hours later and eat him from the inside out. Alice wondered when they might try for a child. She asked Geoff when the time might be right for such an attempt. Geoff choked on a section of burnt cheese and coughed out, "Didn't I mention that I hate kids?"

"That you hate them?"

"I went too far there. Let me dial it back a little. I can't stand them. I've mentioned that in the past. Haven't I?"

"No, you failed to mention that part."

"Is that a deal-breaker?" he said. "I hope not. Because I sure as hell can't go back to Annabelle at this point."

Alice threw her side plate at him, along with a string of expletives trailing closely behind.

Geoff and Alice were not doing fine.

I dropped in on Don and Nancy Greene. They were also having dinner. Don had ordered Nancy's favourite Thai delivery for the occasion. The occasion was this: Don was about to tell Nancy that he had met a most excellent, strapping man, that they were in love, and that he was leaving. He wondered when the timing might be right for the announcement, and if he should leave out the part where the guy was ten years his junior. Nancy, deep in the process of devouring the green curry chicken, hadn't stopped talking about their upcoming annual summer barbecue. A dash of "who had been invited this year" and a main course of "who hadn't." With great delight, she revelled in the pros and cons of each decision, the importance of each name on that list, and the local societal ramifications of those who had been left off it. This went on until the Thai dinner was completely gone.

"You should add one more to the list for the party," said Don.

"Not a chance. We're full and can't handle one more. Not one."

"His name is George, and we've been intimate for the last three weeks. I think he should be invited, if I'm paying for the barbecue. Don't you?"

Don was doing just fine.

Nancy, not so much.

I dropped in on Reverend Rundle as he surfed the web for images of "women's feet," "pics of pedicured toes," and "breast-feeding movie video instructional." There weren't many thought projections to follow in this case. He was pretty much dialled in on the task at hand.

As far as he was concerned, he was doing just fine.

I dropped in on Bob the Bully as he sat in the doctor's office taking in the news that the melanoma had reached his lymphatic system, and more invasive surgery was now required. Bob wondered why they couldn't just grow more skin for him.

"Why not just grow me some new skin?" he said.

"We can't do that," said the specialist. "And that's really not the concern here. The concern is with your lymphatic system."

"You can clone a goddamn sheep, and you're telling me you can't grow me back some new skin? I'll sue everyone in this damn place if you don't at least try. I swear."

Bob the Bully wasn't doing so great.

I hovered over Uncle Phil as he wrote in his diary behind bars. He imagined a dozen different ways he could have sold that last kilo of marijuana without getting caught. He wondered why he had ever agreed to deliver the small amount of cocaine as well. He tore out the page he was writing, crumpled it into a ball, and tossed it to join the fraternity of a dozen or so crumpled paper balls on the floor. He wiped a tear from his eyes and wrote this at the top of a fresh page: *I'm not even upset with myself for what I did. I'm just furious with myself that I got caught. That is the truth. I broke the law. I deserve to serve. I can only improve on myself from here. Tomorrow is a new day.*

He set down the pen and stared at those words for a long while.

Uncle Phil was doing just fine.

Finally, I dropped in on Cathy Anne Frank. She was combing the long, glistening hair of her daughter. The daughter sat cross-legged on the living room floor reading a story aloud from a magazine. Cathy Anne paid no attention to the words, let alone the story. She just focused on combing that hair to perfection, as she had promised she would do back in that shed where she was all tied up. She wondered why a couple of exploratory teenagers had broken into that shed and found her. *Why that particular shed?* she thought. She wondered why the teenage girl with the scraggly red hair and pimply face had demanded to check her pulse, especially given that the teenage boy had promised she was dead, and that they should run. She thought that it didn't matter much now. She was alive for a reason, and at that moment, the reason was to do nothing more than run the teeth of the brush north to south, north to south, creating perfect, vertical lines in her daughter's silken hair.

"Isn't that amazing?" said the daughter. "Can't you just picture it?"

"It's amazing, sweetie."

Cathy Anne was doing just fine.

. . .

After my visit with Cathy Anne, I called for my mentor Rob Sutherland to meet me on top of the Hoover Dam, and he showed up only a few seconds later.

"Kiddo!" he said. "Been a while."

"Been a while, indeed."

"Can you believe all of this action? Pretty wild, isn't it?"

"It is."

"Quite a time to be a ghost," he said, and uploaded to me all of the executions he had witnessed. I ran through all of them in short order.

They all brought back memories.

"That last one I was there for first-hand. I'd been following the story for months, and I knew things were getting heated. Of course, by now humans had been dropping dead all over the place, but the word hadn't spread yet. In this case, it sure hadn't reached these characters, and I managed to catch the whole thing as it went down. I was there when the son of a bitch dropped. I swear it."

Rob was referring to an earthly drama regarding two rival tow-truck companies based out of Richmond Hill. The first company, Get Toad, was owned and operated by Pete Curtis and his brother Dave. The two brothers had two black three-quarter-ton trucks boasting the head and torso of a voluptuous toad named Delilah. Delilah had huge Disney eyes with long lashes and ruby red lipstick. She also wore a red tube top, which she filled out nicely. Bold lettering under Delilah read, NEED TO GET TOAD?

Here's how it all started.

After a night of drinking, Pete came up with the idea for the two brothers to quit their unreliable construction jobs and venture out on their own. Both had high-end pickup trucks due to their involvement in the construction world, so the cost to retrofit those trucks into proper tow trucks wasn't going to kill them in start-up costs. Dave agreed, because that's what Dave did.

They clinked beer bottles. And just like that, Get Toad was born.

Two months later, Delilah 1 and Delilah 2 were retrofitted and on the road. Business began to steadily increase. A few weeks after that, everyone knew about Get Toad and the phone was ringing off the hook.

Delilah and the brothers were a major hit.

However, market research is not something to be overlooked, and what caught the brothers by surprise was the fierce, and often violent, competition in the tow-truck business. In cases where two or three rival tow-truck companies would show up at the same wreck, arguments and fist fights would routinely break out as to who was there first and, ultimately, who would win the tow.

Winning the tow was everything.

That was where Dave Curtis shone.

Some people are tailor-made to fulfill certain roles in this world, and this is what Dave Curtis was made to do — win brawls at the scene of car accidents and breakdowns. Grinning and bloodied, he would win the tow, hook up the cars, and haul them off to the wrecking yard or auto body shops. Dave hadn't felt adrenaline like this since junior hockey where he played the role of enforcer for the team. Moreover, he hadn't filled a role for a long time and was beaming proud to be successfully moving the needle for his company.

Soon, Pete and Dave were household names in the tow truck community, Pete for this brains and gift of the gab, Dave for his muscle. And in flowed the money. Money like the two brothers had never seen before or imagined.

Life had never been better for Pete and Dave. One night, late in the garage, Pete thanked his brother for being such a poor skater but for having such wonderful fists.

"Honestly, man. The NHL is good and all. But I'm having so much fun working with you on this. Everything happens for a reason. This is it, man. I hope you're happy too, brother."

Dave thanked Pete for giving him back his confidence and for making him part of something he could be proud of. A hug was shared, complete with the required harsh slaps on the back and choking down of tears well before surfacing.

The other tow-truck company in this story is Pinky Tows. Pinky Tows was owned and operated by a former biker, Clark Dunleavy, who started a business upon his release from prison fifteen years ago. During his time behind bars, a group of rival inmates had cornered him in the laundry area and pulled both of Clark's pinky fingers from his hands while trying to get information. No information was given by Clark during all of that gruelling tearing and snapping, and what is one to do with no information and two pinky fingers? The pinkys were flushed down the toilet, and Clark had the jagged, hanging skin where his pinkys used to be sewn up hours later by the prison doctor.

After that horrific experience, Clark was known as Pinky.

And it became known that if you were going to get information from Pinky, you'd have to do a hell of a lot more than rip his fingers off.

Since incorporation, Pinky had dominated the tow-truck business for many years, and the dozen or so companies that also existed in that area did so by taking the jobs that Pinky Dunleavy either passed on or was too busy to attend to. Part of this was due to Pinky's noted affiliation with bikers. Part of this was due to the fellow ex-cons he hired to man the trucks, men who had no trouble duking it out to win tows at the scene of an accident. Of course, things began to change when Pete and Dave entered the market and rendered Pinky's hired muscle useless. For the life of them, Pinky's bruisers couldn't beat Dave in a battle of fists. Not if their lives depended on it — which I'll get to later.

By the time the police showed up at the scene of the accident, Dave would have won the fight and the Pinky Tows trucks would be driving off into the distance in a cloud of defeat. The cops would ask Dave if Pinky's boys were giving him any trouble, and Dave would smile, a thin layer of blood covering his teeth and say, "No trouble at all, Officer."

Naturally, these kinds of stories made Pinky angry. They affected his bottom line.

One night, Pinky brought his team of drivers together and announced that they were going to pay Get Toad a visit. He handed out knives and bats and encouraged his drivers to ensure that Pete and Dave got the message. A few of the drivers didn't want any part of it. A few of them had only been released from jail a few weeks ago, and weren't eager to be back behind bars. A few others had been properly tuned up by Dave a few days prior, and their broken noses were still stuffed with gauze.

One threatened to quit.

"If any of you pussies don't want to participate or want to quit," said Pinky, "the bats and knives will be headed your direction instead. That's not a threat. That's a fucking promise."

Dave was washing down Delilah 2 in the garage while Pete worked on the company books in the corner under an old banker's light. As Dave sprayed the soap off Delilah's massive face, he wondered where he might take his family on vacation. He had never been on vacation and pictured his wife and two kids running down an exotic beach, splashing in the waves. He imagined his wife demanding that he and the kids put on sunscreen and refusing the sunscreen just so people back home would ask where he got such a terrible sunburn. This was so he could say, "Aruba. Ever been? It's beautiful." Dave wondered if he should buy something nice for his wife now that he was making good money. He went back and forth between a nice dinner out versus a gift.

Maybe both.

She sure deserves both, he thought. *She sure loved me way before I was a kick-ass tow-truck-driving business owner.*

Pete crunched numbers and wondered how they could save on fuel. He wondered if the trucks they had would last three more years and then compared the maintenance costs of older trucks to the financing costs of a new fleet. He wondered when might be the right time to tell Dave that he wanted to grow the business instead of paying themselves a higher salary. He wondered how Dave might react to that news, given that he'd been talking about fancy vacations for his family and a new house. Would he understand the need to grow the business? Would Dave work well with new members of the team? These questions spun around Pete's head until he heard the smashing. The smashing turned out to be the lights and windshield of Delilah 1, parked outside.

Pete stood up. Dave stopped spraying.

Pinky Dunleavy entered the shop with six of his crew.

"Knock, knock!" said Pinky. Pete ran to Dave's side. He thought they might just go away if he threatened to call 911. Dave recognized the smell of a fight. He knew they were in serious trouble but didn't want to alarm Pete. He knew this visit meant broken bones and months of recovery. But he was set to do his best and minimize the injuries.

"Listen, I'll call 911 if you and your boys don't leave. We'll call it even on the damage so far. Just leave," said Pete. Pinky swung his bat and crushed the taillights on Delilah 2.

"What about now? Or has too much damage been done?" said Pinky. One of Pinky's men ran his knife through the decal of Delilah's face. Another took a bat to Delilah's torso, where the red tube top met the toad's heaving bosom.

Dave stepped in front of Pete, his jaw and fists clenched.

"Here's the deal, guys," said Pinky. "Pete, I admire your work ethic and creativity. Dave, I admire your right hook, which has gotten the better of all of my boys. With skills like that, you should be fighting for a medal at the Olympics, not for Get fucking Toad."

"I'm serious about calling the cops. I have the phone right here. Just leave and we'll call it even," said Pete, whose voice was now audibly trembling.

"Tell you what, boys. We're going to work away at your trucks a little more first. You know, so they have some trouble turning over tomorrow morning. And then we're going to do a little batting practice on the both of you. But we will leave after that on the condition that you boys play by the rules from now on. That you tow what's left for you or what's given to you. Understand?"

"Yes," said Pete. "We understand. Just leave."

Dave turned to Pete, as if betrayed by Judas himself. As if knifed in the back by Brutus.

"No," said Dave. "That's a shitty deal. 'Cause then our trucks are screwed and our bodies are all banged up and then I don't go to Aruba and get a sunburn. So here's the new deal: how about you and your boys bugger off before anyone gets hurt."

With that, Dave raised the spray nozzle on the hose, pulled the trigger, and sent a laser beam of water into Pinky's worn-leather face. Due to the high pressure of the nozzle, a great deal of water made its way into Pinky's mouth and nasal cavities. Pinky coughed and sputtered for several seconds after Dave had stopped with the hosing.

"If your crew wants to win some tows, they'd better take some boxing lessons or learn to play fair like the rest of us," said Dave. "I tell all of these skinny pricks of yours I don't want to fight. They all want to be heroes, these ones."

Pinky, wildly embarrassed at this point, dropped his baseball bat to the floor. It bounced around as bats do, head and toe, head and toe, before settling down and rolling away.

"Nobody disrespects me like that, boys," said Pinky. "That's a death sentence." He drew a gun from a holster inside his leather jacket and pointed it at Dave. "This visit could have been about broken trucks and bones. Maybe a knife in the gut to embrace the spirit of friendly competition. Who knows. Puppy stuff. But then you went and made it about this." He waved the gun to punctuate his point. "So this is really your own fault for being so goddamn stupid."

And up popped the Thought Marker.

Pinky trained the gun on Dave and held the moment, hoping to see Dave squirm or break. But nothing happened.

Dave just stood there, holding his breath.

So Pinky thought, *Oh well*, and squeezed his index finger, which in turn applied pressure to the trigger. Pete Curtis threw himself in front of Dave to intercept the forthcoming bullet, but Pinky stood mystified. The weight of the gun became too much for his limp hand, and he collapsed to the floor. The blood from his eyes, ears, and nose promptly mixed with the soap suds on the garage floor and joined hands with them on their journey toward the drain.

The scene stood still.

Pinky's right-hand man, Griff Stewart, flashed his knife in the air and came screaming toward Pete and Dave, only to suffer the same fate seconds later. He rag-dolled to the concrete floor beside Pinky and emptied his life matter into the drainage system as well.

The rest of Pinky's crew dropped their weapons and slowly backed out of the garage. The pitter-patter of sprinting feet was heard for ten seconds or so.

And then it was all uncomfortably silent.

Ninety-three seconds of silence, in fact.

Not a peep out of them.

That was until Dave put his arms around his brother and tightly squeezed him into the meat of his own thick torso.

"You were going to take that bullet for me, huh."

"I guess I was," said Pete. "But it looks like you have some higher protection than little ol' me."

"Always knew I did, big brother. Always knew it." Dave pointed to the roof of the garage. "The big guy wants us out there towing trucks and making bucks. Plain and simple."

Dave stacked the bodies so he could get to work fixing the damaged Delilahs.

Rob saw me finish the upload and vibrated like crazy. He sent me a questionnaire as to what I thought of the story, and I got to filling it out.

"I was right there hovering in that garage the moment that all went down," he said. "Highlight of my ghosting life, man. Honestly."

He uploaded my questionnaire responses and quickly surmised that I wasn't all that impressed.

"Okay, fine then, Luke. You share with me one story better. I dare you."

So I did.

I sent him every single kill.

I uploaded to him the entirety of my dealings with Safia — up to and including the creation and execution of Operation Stopgap.

"How's that for a trump card?" I said. Rob gave off a strange vibration and didn't respond. "I wasn't impressed with your story of Pete and Dave because I was the one who categorized Pinky Dunleavy's Thought Marker and sent his coordinates for execution. Although the back-story was interesting. Thanks for the share."

"Jesus, Luke. I was sure that all this was on account of the Bookkeeper or What's Next. But this is just another ghost doing all this?" he said.

Given what I had just shared, I asked how he could possibly think that Safia was "just another ghost." He sent me the image of a trucker hat that read, "Fair Enough, Amigo."

"How is that possible?" he said.

"I'm not sure, to be honest."

"Ghosts can't do that. It says so right in the *Handbook*!"

"She gets around it. She's not like us, Rob. She's angry. She's terribly angry, and she vibrates differently because of it. The Line failed her. The whole system failed her."

"This is bad. This is really bad," he said, and I could feel from the vibration he was giving off that he meant it. I could actually feel his fear rising and falling as he used Perspective from his time in the Line to level out his emotions.

"Why is it so bad?" I said, playing a card from Safia's hand. "The world is a safe place. It's a better place. Right?"

"It's not so much what's happened so far that scares me, Luke. It's that kind of power that has me worried for the future."

16

Located to the southwest of roaring London, England, is the county of Surrey. Inside the county of Surrey rests the village of Great Bookham. Just a stone's throw from there, you'll find the charming village of Little Bookham. And while nearly every village in the United Kingdom boasts an old church and an infamous pub to lay its pride upon, Little Bookham also housed one of the world's top mediums, Catherine Seymour. Catherine lived in a humble stone house off Lower Road with her chow, Penelope. This was the kind of stone house where you find moss growing on the tile roof and vines climbing up to make friends with it. You find an active chimney billowing smoke year round and a cobblestone path leading up to the humble cottage made from the same stones you would find in the foundation of the house.

Seventy-one years old seemed young to Catherine, but you'd never be able to place her age unless she told you. Her thin face was too small for the horn-rimmed glasses she wore — given to her by a friend in the process of dying forty years ago. Her friend, Mabel Brighton, suggested that if Catherine wore her glasses, Mabel might be able to see the world from beyond the grave. Catherine didn't know if it was the glasses or the deep grief due to the passing of her best friend, but after she put those horn-rimmed glasses on, she was able to feel the vibrations and receive whispers from the deceased.

After that, they became a permanent fixture.

Where many around the world were not, Catherine was the real deal.

For years, people came from all over the world to visit Little Bookham and the mossy old cottage off Lower Road. People would sit on her antique sofa, drink her tea, and listen as Catherine did her best to decode the vibrations, energy, and images being uploaded to her.

Sometimes what came out of her mouth blew people away.

Sometimes they wept.

Sometimes they laughed right out loud.

Sometimes they heard what they expected to hear, and sometimes the messages were shocking. At times, mortifying.

Either way, Catherine was simply exercising her gift and doing her job to the best of her ability. It was something she took great pride in.

• • •

Exactly one calendar week after my argument with Safia, she called me to the living room of Catherine Seymour. Catherine was in the middle of a session, and Safia and I could feel the vibrations of other ghosts in the room.

"I'm seeing a man," said Catherine.

"Yes," said the woman on the couch. Her name was Marielle Phillipe.

"He's not an old man. He seems young. I'm seeing the number forty-one."

"Yes, that's right. He would have been forty-one this year."

"I'm seeing the initials P and J. Is that right? Do you know someone with those initials?" said Catherine, and Marielle put her hands to her mouth in an attempt to stop an outburst. Her quivering lip certainly wasn't going to be enough. She gathered herself moments later.

"Yes, that's right. That's him. Pierre Joseph. Well, those are his first and middle names."

"I'm seeing a ring. The image of a band. This is your husband."

"Yes, that's him," she said, wiping tears from her eyes. "Is he really here?"

"He's certainly here, dear. And, I must say, from the vibration he's throwing off, he's rather excited about it." Marielle smiled and nodded.

"Good. That's good. I'm excited."

"He has a message for you."

"Yes?"

"I'm getting a dial. A turning dial on a square, and the square is giving off a tremendous amount of heat. Just a second," Catherine said, lowering her chin to her right clavicle. She rotated her head in circles a few times until a smile broke out on her serious face. "My dear, I believe he's asking me to tell you to turn off the stove. Is that right? That can't be right." Marielle, despite the tears, burst into a combination of laughing and crying.

"That's what he's saying, is he?"

"It seems that way, yes," said Catherine, with a greater degree of certainty. "How odd. Did you by chance leave the stove on before you left to journey all this way to see me? If so, you should call someone immediately. We can pause this session."

Marielle shook her head as she collected herself. She rubbed her engagement ring and wedding band with her thumb of the same hand.

"About six months ago, I left the stove on, as I had done time and time again. He was always after me about it. Anyway, I left the stove on after heating some quiche for the kids before school. Many hours later, Pierre walked in the back door from work and closed the back door hard. Not that he was irritated; the frame was a bit off, so you really have to slam it. Well, that slam shook the house a great deal, and this time, the movement in the walls caused an old exposed wire in the circuitry to touch a nail, and, well, there wasn't much left of the house … or Pierre, for that matter." Marielle welled up again after an attempt to keep going with the story, and the knot in her throat formed a blockade preventing any more words from escaping.

"Then it's settled, Marielle. I do believe Pierre is trying to tell you that you should have turned off the bloody stove," Catherine said with a twinkle in her eye and a disarming smile. Marielle went from tears back to hysterical laughter once again.

"He is. I know he is. That's exactly what he's saying."

"I'm seeing white light now, and that means healing and for-giveness. He's telling you to stop carrying the guilt with you. He is happy now."

"I will try my best. Please tell him I will try my best."

"He can hear you. He's likely sitting right beside you."

Marielle looked to the vacant seat cushion beside her and smiled.

"I see children. Three of them."

"Yes. Three. Exactly. Pasha, Pierre Jr., and Pascale."

"He's happy watching over you and your three children," said Catherine, and Marielle made a hard move back to tears. Catherine stood and made her way over to the couch. She sat down beside Marielle and rubbed her back. She sat there rub-bing her back for twenty-three minutes straight. The truth was, Marielle had been feeling better thirteen minutes into the backrub, but loved the healing hands of Catherine Seymour. She sat there and let Catherine rub away, as if she were magically pulling the worm of guilt out through her spine.

Safia vibrated and moved closer to me. I felt that same warmth I had experienced before, as if being covered by a wool blanket.

"You rattled me with your logic," she said.

"Which logic was that?" I said, and she sent me back the image of the Earth with a Band-Aid wrapped around it.

"Yes, well, I may have been a tad harsh. I was frustrated."

"You are right, Luke. What happens when a religious nut or mentally disturbed individual acts out, and I am no longer there to stop it? The world will revert back to the way it was. Perhaps worse."

Safia's vibration grew stronger as her anger multiplied.

Catherine stopped rubbing Marielle's back as the walls shook. The headshot of a former pet, a schnauzer named Bolt, fell from the wall. The glass broke in the frame.

"What was that?" said Marielle.

"I'm not sure," said Catherine, but she knew exactly what it was. "Maybe just a tremor of some kind."

"It's not Pierre, is it?"

"No, I can assure you it's not Pierre. He left about twenty minutes ago."

Safia travelled around the room in circles, her thought projections moving quickly. "If my actions are nothing more than a scare tactic and Band-Aid, if I can't be here to ensure that acts of violence won't continue when I am gone, then I must do my best to change humanity from the inside out."

"To say I'm not following would be a significant understatement."

"Luke, I need to change the thought patterns of human beings from the inside out. Essentially, I need to breed out violent thinking," she said. I asked her to confirm her choice of wording, and she promptly sent back a check mark. Having lived the life of many scientists in the Post-Death Line, I understood that when attempting to breed out a specific trait from any species, it would, by nature, require the discarding of those who didn't meet the criteria. Thus, the discarded are no longer be able to breed and pass the trait along. If the trait was recessive, those discarded might not amount to many. If dominant, the discarded would amount to the majority of the species. Panic settled in quickly and meaningfully.

"Safia, my Band-Aid comment was not intended to inspire further actions against humanity. We've done enough. There's no more work to be done. It was just a comment on the longevity of the operation."

"Luke, you made perfect sense. In fact, you may have salvaged all of our work to date, so as not to be in vain; so as not to be a Band-Aid, as you so aptly put it. Humanity doesn't need a Band-Aid at all. Humanity needs surgery."

I sent her a cartoon version of me placing earplugs into canals. Sound-deadening headphones were then added overtop. The cartoon version of me shrugged his shoulders, and a thought bubble appeared over his head. It read: "Sorry, I can't hear a godforsaken thing."

"Luke, Operation Stopgap is now a three-phase process, and I will be requiring your help once again. Phase One was a tremendous success, and we carried it out to perfection. Those caught in the act of committing violent crimes were removed from the planet, and we managed to bring violent crime to a halt entirely. Phase Two will involve the execution of those who have committed or ordered acts of violence in the past. And by 'in the past,' I mean before Operation Stopgap commenced."

"Safia, Phase Two is redundant. Previous offenders are incapable of reoffending under Operation Stopgap," I said.

"Why should offenders of the past be granted the gift of life? Allowing them to live only rewards the very timing of their offences, and I am not here to reward violent criminals. I am here to get rid of them. Moreover, in changing the human thought process at a cellular level, I must dispose of past offenders so they cannot further procreate."

"You're actually bringing procreation into this?"

"Reproduction is a process of sharing traits. I am not prepared to risk violent Thought Traits from being passed down."

"This feels more like a thirst for blood than change," I said. Safia disagreed and requested that she be allowed to finish before any judgments were made. I sent her an apology letter, signed and dated at the bottom. She sent me back a document formally accepting the apology.

"Like I said, Phase One is complete, and Phase Two is about removing violent criminals from the past, entirely. Phase Three involves the termination of anyone caught thinking about seriously injuring, maiming, raping, or killing another individual."

I sent her the image of the Grand Canyon with a Las Vegas–style neon sign that read, "Grand Canyon Cemetery" and asked if she thought it might be big enough to hold the number of dead bodies that were sure to pile up.

"This is a process of cleansing the human race, and there will be casualties, Luke. I can assure you of it. There are going to be millions and millions of casualties. Possibly billions," she said and returned my image of the Grand Canyon Cemetery, having added the words "No Vacancy" in the same flashing neon lettering. The *V* flickering in and out.

"You can't execute humans for what they think!"

"Why not? Thoughts manifest actions, do they not?"

"They do, but ..."

"And do we not use Thought Markers to prevent violent crimes from taking place?"

"We do, but that's because the thought in question has reached a level whereby action is the decision."

"Exactly, it all starts with the thought. And to your wonderful point, in order to do everything I can to prevent the return of violence, I must rip off the Band-Aid and perform surgery on the human race in order to change it once and for all."

I sent her the image of a luxury yacht with the name, "Gone Overboard" written on the hull in calligraphy.

"Stop it," she said. "I have not."

"To execute humans based on violent thoughts is to charge them with the crime of being what they are: intelligent animals. What makes humans different is the power of choice. Thoughts enter minds, and humans have the ability to choose whether to let those thoughts become actions. To execute them for the thought alone is a crime against humanity. And you know it. Listen, I've gone along with this mandate of yours so far because innocent lives have been saved in the process. People are safe now where they weren't before. But this is too much. This is murder, Safia," I said, and sent her a document she was required to sign and acknowledge that Phase Three was murder in the first degree.

She sent back the document aflame.

"My hypothesis is this: those who survive Phase Three are likely to breed and raise children who are less likely to have violent thoughts, and the process will continue until it becomes a dominant trait in humanity. So much so that even the mentally ill won't consider acts of violence."

"Exactly," I said. "It's a wild hypothesis based on zero factual evidence that will result in the death of hundreds of millions of innocent people."

"Perhaps," she said. "I am doing the best I can with the time I have."

"When are these phases set to commence?"

"I will attempt to give a degree of warning to the people of the world. My plan is to have Catherine Seymour play messenger and make a global announcement. First, she will clear up any misconceptions surrounding who or what is responsible for the acts of intervention; that they are, in fact, the actions of a ghost who will patrol the Earth until the end of time. The last half of that section is technically a lie, but I will have her say it anyway. In the second section of her announcement, she will deliver the exact details surrounding Phase Two and Phase Three. Phase Two will commence twenty-four hours after the announcement, Phase Three one year later. Hopefully that will give people enough time to change their thinking patterns."

"Having Catherine reveal who is responsible feels more like an attempt to gain notoriety than part of a higher plan."

"Not at all. Humanity needs to stop thinking that God is involved, since anything faith-based can get twisted and misinterpreted. I want to put a definitive end to certain debates. I want the world to know that there is a ghost watching over them, forever and ever. Amen.

That an entirely agnostic ghost, unrelated to any theology, or religious belief system is dedicated to human improvement at any cost."

"This won't end religion, if that's what you're thinking."

"Agreed, but it might prevent one from thinking that their god will protect them, should they act out against the rules. This is to save lives, Luke. Not to gain notoriety."

"And what if Catherine Seymour disagrees?"

"To what?"

"To be your vessel. Your messenger."

"We've been communicating for days. She's on board."

Safia sent me the full transcript of their back and forth over the past weeks, up to and including yesterday afternoon.

We paused to watch Catherine Seymour show Marielle to the door. Marielle wrote the cheque and thought it wasn't enough. Catherine accepted the cheque and thought it was too much. The two women hugged, and Marielle was soon on her way to the cab that was waiting at the end of the cobblestone walkway.

Safia hovered close to me. I sent her a video clip of two magnets with the same charge coming close to one another, and the predictable distancing. One magnet read "Safia." The other, "Luke."

"Are these acts of yours the acts of a hero?" I said. "I thought that was the role you were playing."

"Sometimes heroes have to make difficult decisions. That's what makes them heroes, isn't it?"

"When does the hero, in an effort to do good, become the villain?" I said and sent her a famous quote by Friedrich Nietzsche with respect to monsters.

"When the hero abandons the big picture," she said.

I uploaded to her a stylized image of the word "hero" so that the letters were wrought with cracks and fractures.

I left and hovered over the Eiffel tower, looking onto the city of lights. *How many of these lights are going to be extinguished a year from now?* I wondered.

17

Catherine Seymour sat in the face of the bright studio lights. A young woman from the make-up department powdered her forehead and cheeks while another glossed her lips. A middle-aged man from the sound department fussed with the lavalier microphone hidden under a fold on the collar of her blouse.

"Can you speak for me, ma'am?" he said.

"What would you like me to say?"

"Oh, any old thing. Just count to ten if you wish."

So she did. She counted to ten and then counted to ten three more times as the sound team made final adjustments.

A woman from the lighting crew asked Catherine to rotate slightly to her left. Then the make-up girls came back to do more touch-ups, since the new angle had surfaced some oily patches.

"These lights are quite hot, aren't they, Mrs. Seymour?" said one of the girls caking on the powder.

"They are, indeed. I'm catching quite the glow here, aren't I?" she said, and wondered whether, if she cracked an egg on the black granite of the polished news desk, might it fry. She played this action out in her head — dressed in chef's attire, cracking a dozen

eggs on the news desk and asking those around her how they preferred them to be cooked. In her mind, one of the make-up girls
asked for scrambled and was promptly scolded, given that scram-
bling was, indeed, no proper way to treat a perfectly good egg.

"It's fine, ma'am. That's what we're here for," said the make-up girl.

"Pardon me, dear. What is it that you are here for? I was off in
another world."

"To make sure you aren't shiny on camera. You know, given the
heat of the lights."

"Of course. Yes. You're doing a fine job, I'm sure," said Catherine,
although part of her still held an irrational grudge due to the girl's
imaginary penchant for scrambled eggs. She thought that was silly
and unfair but couldn't help it — the same way one holds a grudge
when wronged by someone in a bad dream.

Catherine wondered how professional news people put up with
this for a living — all the doctoring and fussing and lights and micro-
phones with wires running from your clavicle to a device velcro'd
around your ankle. She wondered how her announcement would go,
and if this was, in fact, a terrible idea. Would she go down in history
as a saint or as some sort of witch or devil? Someone that just a few
hundred years before would have been strapped to the dunking chair,
boiled in a pot, or burned at the stake. She thought she certainly
would have been and was thankful for the timing of it all. Certainly,
messengers of higher thinking hadn't fared so well in the past. *Don't
kill the messenger*, she thought, but killing was obviously out of the
question with Safia around. *Here come my fifteen minutes of fame*, she
thought, and that made her feel sick to her stomach.

Catherine swallowed the ounce of bile that had been brought up
with a burp. *How embarrassing*, she thought, *to vomit all over myself
after this level of fussing*. She imagined herself vomiting all over the
news desk and herself, and the two pretty make-up girls doing their
final touches. The first daydream was the kind of vomiting where
you can't quite control it and it spurts out of clenched jaws, failing

in the attempt to hold it back. In this case, bearing the brunt of it. However, the second daydream showcased projectile vomiting wherein everyone within ten feet of her sightline was affected by direct spray or splash. Both daydreams were followed by Catherine saying, "Pardon me. I'm very sorry. What a mess I've made."

Fame was the last thing she had ever wanted. Attention at a dinner party was too much for her to bear. However, this announcement, this news and media event, was for the greater good, she told herself. It would save lives. And that went well beyond Catherine Seymour from Little Bookham and her hang-ups with attention and notoriety.

To her, this was a matter of duty.

When the world-famous anchor Sterling MacKinnon sat down next to Catherine at that world-famous news desk, her heart rate increased. This announcement was sure to happen in short order. The make-up, sound, and lighting departments descended upon Sterling for final touches. He sat there with his eyes closed and let it all take place, like a trained show dog being groomed to run around the competition ring. His heart rate, too, was elevated as he understood the full significance of what was about to happen. That today's exclusive with Catherine Seymour would be the most important piece of world news he would ever be a part of. That this interview would go down in history and be shown to classrooms around the world for generations to come. At least, that was what his producer had told him thirty minutes ago. Sterling sat there as the powder brushes tickled his nose and forehead, marinating in the moment he had been waiting for his entire lifetime — his moment of immortalization.

Final touches wrapped up.

Lighting was set.

Sound crews were ready and cameras were up.

A man with bulky headphones covering his ears and holding a clipboard began to loudly count down from four.

"In four, three two," he said, dropping the corresponding fingers along the way. When the time came to yell "one," he was silent. He held that sole index finger up in the air, and then that finger began to circle wildly in a helicopter motion.

Safia and I hovered over the news desk. She controlled her vibration patterns so as not to disrupt the lights or sound equipment.

"This is it," she said.

I sent her a clip of a speeding car that had lost the ability to brake.

What follows is a transcription of the interview.

18

"Good evening. I'm Sterling MacKinnon. For just under three months now, the world has done its best to adapt and make sense of the wave of executions associated with miraculous acts of intervention and interference in the face of violence crimes. Debates have raged as to who or what may be responsible for these actions, but even the most compelling hypotheses by top theologians, scientists, and philosophers have been just that, nothing more than a slew of best guesses in an attempt to explain seemingly unexplainable acts. Today we have with us celebrated medium Catherine Seymour, who, right now, is making her first on-air appearance to deliver a message and some insight into who or what is responsible for what's been going on. Catherine, it's a pleasure to have you with us today."

"Thank you."

"Before we really get into it, Catherine, how is it that you are able to connect to those trapped in the afterlife as ghosts?"

"First of all, I'm not so sure they're all trapped. However, yes, I am able to connect with spirits and accept information from them through the decoding of symbols, letters, and other means of communication."

"So, to be clear, it's not a true discourse you have with ghosts. Like we're having right now."

"No, not like we're having right now. But yes, it is a true discourse. It is a language that I have the ability to both intercept and decode. I then relay that information on to others."

"What do you say to those who feel all this is just a big hoax? That you have no powers at all? That this is just a way to take the money of hard-working people and tell them what they want to hear."

"I would suggest those people come and see me. Many have done this over the years. The non-believers sit down on my comfy sofa, and I tell them things about themselves and loved ones I couldn't possible know. I relay messages from any friends or loved ones who have chosen to attend the session in spirit form. And those non-believers, they change their minds pretty quickly about what I do. Many of them become repeat clients."

"Does that mean we all have family members or friends as ghosts who want to deliver a message?"

"No, in the case where there is not a family member or friend present, there is always a spirit hanging around my living room. They're just drawn there, I suppose, and they can share with me the thoughts of those sitting in front of me. Sometimes all people want to hear are their own thoughts and fears regurgitated to them through another voice. Sometimes that solidifies important decisions for them or simply surfaces the truth."

"So you could do the same to me, or anyone else?"

"Yes, that's correct. That is exactly how I find myself sitting today with you. I had to convince many skeptics along the way to get here."

"That's truly amazing."

"It's only as amazing as a pianist plays the piano or a mathematician solves equations, or a farmer raises crops. It's just what I'm good at. It's my gift to the world. It's the thing that I do well. Nothing more."

"I understand you have an important message to deliver."

"I do."

"And what is that?"

"A couple of months ago I was contacted by a spirit who had an energy vibration pattern unlike anything I had ever been in contact with."

"I just want to be clear that when you say spirit, you mean a ghost."

"I said spirit, so you can draw from that and reclassify it as you wish."

"Understood. Please carry on."

"This spirit came to me and began sending me messages that were crystal-clear in their delivery. Sometimes decoding takes a bit of thought and deduction, but this was advanced. I shouldn't say advanced. This was different, but in a good way for me — the decoder."

"And what did the spirit have to say? This ghost."

"The spirit, a female I might add, took full responsibility for the acts of intervention. She took full responsibility for the executions and asked me to deliver a message to the humans of this planet."

"And what is that message, Catherine?"

"Excuse me, dear. I just need a sip of water. (*coughing*) There. Pardon me."

"It's fine. Take your time."

"She asked me to deliver this message to the people of the world. Here it goes, as best as I can translate: I am watching over this planet and will be performing these acts of intervention until the end of time or of humanity — whichever comes first. I will continue to intercept acts of violence and punish those who attempt to carry out acts of violence with death. Twenty-four hours from now, individuals, convicted or not, who have carried out acts of violence in the past, including sexual assault, physical violence with the intent to severely injure, or murder, will be executed as well. In addition to that, those who have ordered another individual or individuals to carry out the preceding list of crimes in the past shall also face execution by my hand."

"Catherine, I want to pause you here for a second. You are absolutely certain that is the message."

"I am. Yes."

"What you are talking about here could be the deaths of hundreds of thousands of individuals."

"I'm unsure as to the number, but yes. Many."

"Did this female ghost give a reason for her decision in this regard?"

"She didn't think it fair that criminals who have committed past crimes not face the appropriate penalty, as many have since her acts of interference started. Also, she is attempting to rid the idea of violent crime from the human thought pattern, so she didn't want criminals of that nature able to procreate."

"Hold on, Catherine. Please repeat that if you would? She's attempting to do what?"

"I'm getting ahead of myself, but she is attempting to unequivocally rid the human mind of the ability to contemplate violent crimes."

"Through the murder of those who have committed crimes in the past?"

"Partially, through the removal of those who have a history of violence. Yes. That's how I would put it."

"Why did you just say, 'That's how I would put it'? Are these your thoughts, and not the thoughts of the being who is ultimately responsible for these acts?"

"It was a slip. I apologize. That is how I would best translate it."

"Understood."

"Nevertheless, the removal of past criminals is only part of her ultimate plan. There is larger message I am here to deliver."

"Before you do that, Catherine, I would like to repeat the breaking news for all of those tuning in at this time. Those of you who have committed acts of violence in the past, whether convicted or not, have only twenty-four hours to live, based on the information we've gathered here just now. This is Catherine Seymour, world-renowned medium, speaking on behalf of a ghost that we now learn is claiming responsibility for the acts of intervention."

"As I said, that is only part of the message."

"Yes. You mentioned her attempt to rid the human thought pattern of violent crime. What's next after this second purging of criminals?"

"From what she's told me, the next phase, phase three, will involve the execution and removal of individuals who have thoughts of violent crimes. This final phase of her plan is an initiative to rid the human psyche of violent thoughts. This phase will commence in approximately one year's time. She thought that was an ample amount of time for people to mentally prepare."

"Mentally prepare. You mean, stop thinking violent thoughts entirely?"

"Indeed."

"Couldn't one argue that is impossible? That our nature is one that breeds violent thought patterns based on our history of evolution and survival? How are we supposed to change that in one year's time?"

"I'm not sure. I'm only here to deliver the message."

"We're now talking about the potential removal, the potential murder of billions of people for committing thought crimes. Not actual crimes."

"Again, I'm unsure as to the numbers. But yes. Many."

"I just want to clarify. Are we are to rid our minds of violent thoughts or rid our thoughts of violent crimes?"

"I'm not sure. Those who have legitimate thoughts of violent crimes against another human will be executed as per her mandate. She is suggesting that people begin to train their minds to positive thinking, should they wish to survive."

"Brain training? You're kidding."

"This is not a comedy hour. Nor am I a performer here to tell jokes. I am relaying a message from the spirit responsible for all of this, who wants to share with the world the truth about the force responsible for these acts of interference and has chosen me to warn the world with the reality of what is yet to come."

"This all seems quite impossible. Doesn't it?"

"What, over the course of the last three months, has seemed possible to you so far, Sterling?"

"It seemed hopeful that we had someone or something here to protect us from future acts of violence. What you are suggesting is that this female ghost is not only going to punish those who have committed previous acts violence, many of whom have served their time for those crimes, but that she is taking things much further … something that will without question result in the death of innocents. And all of this by a force we had all hoped was here to protect us."

"From what I understand, she is less interested in protecting us and more interested in changing us."

"Alteration is a long way from protection, don't you think?"

"Perhaps."

"I'm only trying to establish whether she is on our side or not."

"Well, what do you think?"

"Candidly, I'm not so sure anymore. We're talking about the murder of innocents due to what could be harmless thought patterns."

"Since when have violent thought patterns been harmless? What good has ever come from such thoughts? She sees it as a flaw in humanity that she actively is going to attempt to resolve."

"And thought crimes, punishable by death, is what we're dealt in an attempt to resolve it."

"Correct."

"I'll ask the question again: How are we supposed to change our natural thought patterns in so little time?"

"You are asking the wrong person."

"Then please ask her. I think I, along with our viewers, am entitled to an answer. Can you ask her?"

"She said that you shouldn't worry about it, Sterling."

"Why's that?"

"Because you only have twenty-four hours to live."

19

Twenty-four hours later, Sterling MacKinnon was dead, as were scores of others. His legacy would be coining the term "Thought Crimes," which Safia wildly approved of. She believed it to be both clever and catchy. She thought that the broadcast effectively delivered her message, and we quickly shifted our focus to building a better mousetrap.

Prior to and during Catherine Seymour's live announcement, I closely monitored the methodology we had developed to log and chart thought patterns the world over. As soon as Catherine made her historic announcement, as soon as individuals heard and digested the news, instinctively they pulled forward any crime they had committed that might qualify for their forthcoming execution. From there, I was able to filter and batch the guilty thoughts accordingly. As the thoughts came in, I marked the guilty with tracer codes, and Safia began her next round of executions. Within twenty-four hours, mostly everyone in the world had either witnessed, listened to, or been told about Catherine's announcement, and within the same amount of time the world was completely rid of the kind of criminal Safia so deeply loathed.

Like the others, they had all fallen, and their faces made a mess of something.

Without question, the world was on its ear. Many governments had laid leaders to rest. Cities and communities had collected the dead. Call and email services were set up should an individual request collection services to gather the body of a family member, loved one, or friend.

Cemeteries were expanded upon or created.

Pits were dug.

People were bulldozed.

In the correctional facilities and military prisons around the globe, many convicted of crimes were found in their jail cells, lifeless and bleeding from the face. At the same time, many in the same prisons convicted of these types of crimes sat there, asking to finally be set free. And they were.

Prisons simply opened their doors. The bars were pulled back, and whoever could walk out was free to do so. And out walked those who could.

Hours before Safia's Phase Two, social media outlets had become the platform for the guilty to share their terrible secrets with the world.

Closets were opened up. Skeletons revealed. Followed by apologies for the crimes that had been committed.

Followed by pleas for forgiveness.

Then goodbyes.

A week after the execution of Phase Two, the world's focus shifted to preparing for Phase Three. Any political and religious debates had been pushed entirely to the side. Instead, motivational speakers in the business of positive thought and brain training now owned the day. As did speech pathologists, who, to combat communication disorders, taught students how to change one's line of thinking in order to communicate effectively. Thus, through the same training used to successfully correcting a stutter, speech pathologists believed they could apply the same technique to the masses and effectively instruct on how to switch up thought patterns to avoid negative and violent thinking. Entire TV channels became dedicated to brain training for the forthcoming purge of humanity.

Mental calisthenics.

Brain gym.

BrainAudible.com, a website streaming videos and interviews with top speech pathologists and motivational speakers, became the most popular, with millions upon millions of hits per day, translated into every language around the world with the click of a button.

ThoughtScrubber.com was another popular site, though it was backed by the Catholic church and exclusively in English. To enter the site, you first had to check a box that stated, "I believe in Jesus Christ, our Lord and Saviour, and have fully accepted him into my heart." Then, after checking this box, you could click "Enter." Thus, by their standards, the process of gaining access to the website was not that dissimilar to that of heaven.

Safia called me to hover over a family of six in Annecy, France, as they huddled around the computer, soaking in the brain exercises and coaching tips to rid the mind of negative and violent thoughts. All six of them working diligently. The mother and father acting as drill sergeants in a speed round of evolution. The children were determined to see another birthday.

Safia loved this. "Look at them," she said. "Look at how dedicated they are to human improvement."

"They seem to be wonderful people."

"Indeed."

"I wonder how many of them will end up in the ground in a year's time."

"Hopefully, not many of them if they keep this kind of training up," she said. I sent her the graphic image of a rattlesnake with all of its biology identified. The top of the chart read, "cold-blooded."

With that, the time was right to do what I'd been mulling over for quite some time. I sent her my formal letter of resignation. Signed and dated at the bottom.

A copy was sent to the Bookkeeper as well.

The letter read as follows.

20

Dear Safia,

Due to your forthcoming crimes against humanity with specific regard to the execution of a considerable percentage of the human race, I hereby resign as your Colonel. Please do not expect any further help, as I refuse to participate in the slaughter of innocents, despite your strong convictions that Phase Three will only strengthen and improve upon the human race. It is my sincere wish that you reconsider your actions.

Sincerely,

Luke James Stevenson

21

To say that Safia was unimpressed with my letter of resignation would be like suggesting that an aggressive bout of food poisoning while in an airplane lavatory was an inconvenience. She vibrated so fiercely that a twelve-hundred-square-kilometre section of ice broke away from the Pine Island Glacier in Antarctica and floated off into the Amundsen Sea. Fault lines around the world rubbed elbows with each other, and news channels hypothesized that the global quake was a potential early warning signal for the commencement of punishable Thought Crimes. That was until a reporter interviewed a New Jersey man who had let his thoughts get the better of him during a fit of road rage. His story went like this:

"I couldn't help it. The guy cut me off, and I had to swerve like this, and then they guy slows right down and I thought, man, I want to kill that guy. I imaged that my car had rocket launchers that rose up out of the hood, like something out of an action film, and launched, and off went the rockets, and, you know, made scrap metal out of his shitty old Honda. God's honest truth, all I thought about was making an organ donor out of him. And then I realized what I done, you know, in thinking that stuff and expected the worst. But it didn't come. So, whatever that means. I guess the girl ghost, I guess she's not offing us for Thought Crimes yet. Lucky for me, right? I'm gonna hug my kids extra tight tonight. You know, play catch with them and all that. Read them books and tuck them in. I would just say to people, maybe stay out of your cars. They can get you into situations where you want to really kill people real bad and put them in the hospital and stuff. Look, I know I won't be driving anymore, that's for damn sure."

Of course, the clip went viral. And the world breathed a sigh of relief.

"You can't resign," said Safia. "There is no way I can monitor the Thought Crimes and carry out the executions as well."

"Then you should have thought of that," and I sent her the cover of a university textbook titled *Business Planning for Business Owners*.

"We had a deal. I have a signed contract from you for Operation Stopgap."

"This is no longer Operation Stopgap. This is something else."

"This is a continuation of Stopgap."

"It's not what I signed up for. Therefore, I'm no longer bound to help."

"This is required!"

"I'm out, Safia. You'll have to find a way to do it yourself."

"The information is too much to process, and when Phase Three commences, I can't miss a Thought Crime. If I do, the whole thing just doesn't work. People can't get away with a few and tell a friend about it. It needs to be swift and real, so the world takes it seriously," she said, and vibrated fiercely.

I sent a clip of a locomotive pulling a thousand cars. Every even numbered car contained oil, and every odd numbered car contained propane. I had the locomotive take a turn too quickly. I had it derail, and the thousand cars behind it jackknifed into one another. Twisted metal sparked, setting off a sequence of explosions a thousand railcars long. The burning aftermath section of the clip was a single-take aerial shot that lasted ninety minutes.

"So we've arrived at this, have we?" I said. "Have you given any thought to the fact that my own family will be affected by this? And yours? Are you prepared to execute your own mother and father … and mine? My sister, who is pregnant, and her fiancé — are all of these people in the crosshairs, Safia?" I sent her the image of a white flag waving atop an old stone castle. The name on the front door of the castle was "Luke's Family." My greatest fear in all of this was that a Thought Crime from a loved one might make its way into the filtering system. Light up the screen and demand of me to send Safia the coordinates to end their thinking, and their lives accordingly.

"Will you be asking that of me, Safia?" And I uploaded to her a form with a list of ten names that would have immunity. A ghastly act of nepotism, no question, but in considering the position, I had to fully understand my benefits package.

"Luke, Phase Three will start in exactly one year's time," she said and sent me a clock counting down the days, hours, seconds, tenths, and hundredths of seconds. "You have between now and then to make up your mind regarding your continued service. The betterment of humanity is a cause I am deeply committed to. That said, for your service, I will allow you one exemption. One person with immunity from Phase Three. You have the pick of the litter, but I know where your allegiance lies. Not likely with your mother or your sister. Though that's not what you want to hear from me. It seems that once again Diana's life rests in your hands," she said and sent me the image of a miniaturized Diana lying in her open palms, as if trying to catch some afternoon sun. Then, hinged at the pinky fingers, Safia's palms snapped together like a bear trap, and the guts and bone of miniaturized Diana oozed from between the fingers. The clip was quite gruesome. I sent her a clip of a simple black line and then had the likeness of Safia crossing it.

"It's entirely up to you," she said. "Your motives for helping are not paramount. Help because we share a vision. Help to save a life. Help, or don't help, and watch it all go down from the bleachers."

22

It was a feeling of complete helplessness. One I hadn't experienced since arriving at the Post-Death Line, or since my marriage to Alice. That feeling where you might as well be at the bottom of a hundred-metre-deep pit with nothing more than a thick, braided rope dangling down to get you out, but you look down and have no hands and no feet for climbing. But you're a fighter, so you try to make do with your arm stubs where hands should be and leg stubs where feet should be, but you simply lack the means by which climbing is possible.

And the rope just dangles there, teasing you. Punctuating your helplessness.

So you shrug and sit down. Call yourself a failure.

In the case of concocting a plan to save Diana's life and to thwart Safia's Thought Crime initiative, that was me at the bottom of the pit with no hands and feet, attempting to climb the rope, armed with all the good intentions of finding a way but slowly drifting into capitulation.

• • •

I met with Rob, and we hovered over a concert venue in Tokyo, Japan, where a specialist in thought training was speaking to a crowd of one hundred and fifty thousand on the importance of releasing anger, letting go, and forgiving those who had wronged you in the past. That this was the only way to prevent violent thoughts from surfacing in the future. The crowd soaked it all in. For those unable to see the event live, it was being streamed live on BrainAudible.com for $29.99.

If a mentor spirit was designed for support and guidance, there was no time like the present. I shared with Rob the predicament du jour, and he said, "You've gotta find a way to stop her."

I sent him over a wax-sealed diploma from Harvard University for his Master's Degree in Stating the Obvious.

He sent me back a middle finger.

"You're my mentor. Isn't it your duty to give me something better than that?"

He sent me a clip of a hand drawing the word "blank" on chalkboard.

"What's the Bookkeeper saying about all of this?" he said. "That's what gets me. She's in clear violation of the code here."

"I've reached out to the Bookkeeper several times, with no response. He's gone silent on me. Perhaps because I've failed so miserably as a Mentor. But it's not for a lack of trying."

Rob sent me a short document. It was the preamble to a story he was about to tell. The preamble read: *I think you might like this story.*

"So I happen upon this scene a while back," he said. "Might have been ten years, but well before you arrived and the world turned upside down. In any case, I'm back in my hometown, floating around, catching up on all the people and the gossip and all that, and I come across six boys in the woods. Two sets of three brothers. One set of brothers, the Hillbigs, and the other set of brothers, the Jays. Hillbigs were older than Jays by a few years, but when we're talking about all of them being under the age of fifteen, a few years is a big deal.

"So the oldest Hillbig, he's ordered his two brothers to pin the two youngest Jay brothers to the ground, leaving the oldest Jay brother to watch from ten or fifteen feet or so. Oldest Hillbig says to oldest Jay, 'I'm going to lay a serious beat-down on one of your brothers, but you have to pick which one gets the beating.' Oldest Jay, now wild with anger and frustrated to the hilt says, 'I'm not making that decision, so if you're going to beat one of us up, just pick one and get it over with.' Oldest Hillbig smiles and says, 'No, you don't get it. I'll beat them both up, if you don't pick one, and the beating I'll give both of them will be worse than the beating I'll give one of them if you don't man up and choose one to receive the beating.' Like an oldest brother would, like a true hero would, oldest Jay says, 'Let both of them go, and give me the beating. That's my decision.'

"But this isn't what the oldest Hillbig has in mind. 'No, that's too easy,' says oldest Hillbig. 'I know it'll hurt you more to have to pick one or watch them both get beaten. So I'm asking you one more time to pick one of your brothers, or they'll both be catching the beating of their lives, right here in front of you while you watch.' Now, imagine that predicament, Luke. Here, the oldest Jay brother isn't armed with the muscle, size, or fighting skills to save his brothers, but he has to find a way to get all three of them out of this mess without picking a brother for the beating, and without both of those younger brothers of his getting harmed in the process. Quite a situation, am I right?"

I sent him a check mark.

"Do you know what the oldest Jay brother did to get one or more of his brothers out of the purported beating of their lives?"

I sent him a question mark.

"This is what oldest Jay says to oldest Hillbig: 'I've heard your stepdaddy beats on you. Is that true?' And oldest Hillbig just looks at him, stunned. He says, 'Choose, Jay. Choose which one gets the beating.' And the oldest Jay says, 'When he's sick of beating on you, does he force you to pick which brother gets the beating?' The oldest Hillbig is rattled by this. Poor bugger didn't see that kind of thing coming — not in a situation like this. He screams at the oldest Jay. He says, 'You have ten seconds to choose, or the both of them get it!' And oldest Jay looks him square in the eyes and says, 'Well, how about I make you a deal? If it's your stepdaddy you really want to be laying the beating on, then let's the six of us right here and now agree to get that done together.' Oldest Hillbig again just stands there perplexed, wrestling with his bruised ego at the shift in power taking place, and playing out in his mind what a beating on his stepdaddy might look like. With all six of them. He plays it ten times over. The only question that remains is whether or not six will be enough to take him.

"And oldest Jay says, 'Yeah, I think the six of us could whip the shit out of him, and easily. But we've gotta be a team, and we've gotta plan how it's going to go down.' And just like that, oldest Hillbig orders his brothers to remove their knees from the spines of the younger Jay brothers, and they all dust off and shake on it. The rest of the day is spent behind the Jay family barn, hashing out a plan to take care of the real issue at hand. That's you, Luke. You're the oldest Jay — faced with an impossible situation and have to surface the real issue at hand in order to win."

23

If I had learned anything from Safia thus far, it was that the realm
of what seemed possible went far beyond the Code of Conduct or
anything in the *Ghosting Handbook*. Certainly, I hadn't been getting
answers from the Bookkeeper, so on a whim, I thought I'd craft a
letter to whoever presides over What's Next. There was nothing
in the Code or *Handbook* suggesting communications beyond the
Bookkeeper, nor did I have an address or coordinates to What's Next.

In what direction was I to send this message?

Was I to hitch it to passing comets — carrier pigeons of the universe?

On second thought, there could be a postman at my fingertips.
Perhaps the Bookkeeper was required by Universal Law to deliver
messages from ghosts to What's Next?

It seemed a stretch but entirely reasonable.

I decided to start there.

My mind was made up to write a letter to What's Next c/o The
Bookkeeper.

A wave of fear flowed over me as to the possible repercussions
for having been involved with Operation Stopgap. If my letter was
to somehow reach What's Next, what might my penalty be for

clearly interfering with what was meant to be, and to the organic evolution of humanity?

Perhaps the best thing to do was keep my mouth shut.

No one likes a whistle-blower.

I had been a whistle-blower once, in the Line. I had lived the life of a deputy director of corporate security for one of the world's largest pharmaceutical companies. It was a high-ranking role that covered a broad range of responsibilities such as anti-product counterfeiting operations, crisis and risk management planning, internal theft, tampering investigations, and conducting site security surveys around the world. With some digging around, outside the realm of my operational mandate, what I had uncovered was that the CEOs and co-founders of the firm had been paying off government officials from developing countries to approve certain drugs that were not ready for the Western market. They weren't ready because they hadn't completed all of the rigorous Western standards for testing. What it all meant was that the firm was looking to start making money on a drug that wasn't safe to be sold, and I blew the whistle and blew it hard. Like many whistle-blowers before me, I was promptly investigated, fired, made an example of, and eventually found myself looking down the barrel of a silencer upon returning home from a full day's hearing on the matter.

"I can only imagine what this is about," I said to the gunman.

"You're about to be the victim of a random and unfortunate burglary," he said. "That's all." Then he pulled the trigger, and that was the end of that life.

Thus, my only experience with whistle-blowing had resulted in the highest form of punishment. If one plus one equals two, what was to be made of me in this situation? How would I be handled by What's Next upon surfacing the single greatest act of spiritual interference in the history of the world?

Would I be a villain or hero?

My thoughts tended toward villain, but dirty hands, by nature, need cleaning. Whatever the punishment, whatever the price, I had been involved in events with incalculable repercussions for humanity and deserved what may come my way. Except this time, the lives of innocents were at stake, which trumped by far my criminal anonymity with respect to the first two phases of Operation Stopgap.

My mind was made up.

Despite unknown consequences, I chose to draft the letter and asked the Bookkeeper to deliver it to What's Next.

24

From: Luke James Stevenson
Spirit Number: 3765 572 5678 563 4874
To: What's Next
c/o The Bookkeeper
Message Status: TIME-SENSITIVE

To Whomever Presides over What's Next,

It is with a great deal of humility, sadness, and grief that I must inform you as to events that have taken place on planet Earth over the last several months, as well as to warn you with regard to events planned for one year's (Earth) time from now.

As per the mentorship program, I was awarded a Recently Delivered Spirit named Safia Jaffi. From the beginning, it was very clear that somehow the Post-Death Line had not provided her proper perspective, nor had the Line eased standard human emotions such as emotional pain, anger, resentment, frustration, and fear.

Only a few weeks after reintegration, Safia informed me about her ability to execute living beings when attempting to connect to them while in an enraged state. Given this newfound, unique ability, Safia promptly developed a system to intercept and prevent all violent crimes on the planet through a mandate she called Operation Stopgap. Through this initiative, many thousands of lives were taken and many thousands more saved. To Safia, this mission was a roaring success. Though the success of the mission was also partly due to my help in the matter.

As her appointed Colonel in Operation Stopgap, I hereby accept responsibility for aiding in a mission that altered what was meant to be — thus breaking the Code that I signed off on prior to my own reintegration.

In accepting responsibility, I also accept any repercussions or punishment that may be associated with such acts.

Moreover, my letter is one of warning. In one year's time, Safia will roll out the final phase of her work as she attempts to alter the human thought pattern. Safia intends to execute any living being guilty of Thought Crimes; that is, the mere act of thinking about committing violent crimes. With all her might, she intends to breed violent thinking out of humanity.

It is my sincere hope that unless Safia's acts are part of what was meant to be, you interfere as soon as possible, before a year's time is up and the execution of innocents commences.

Sincerely,
Luke James Stevenson

25

I submitted the letter to the Bookkeeper with clear instructions to deliver it to What's Next. With the letter, I attached both a delivery and read receipt. The Bookkeeper sent me back two check marks in the corresponding boxes. That marked the first successful interaction I'd had with the Bookkeeper for months.

I wrote back and asked if he would be forwarding the letter.

He informed me that for the second time since he took control of the Post-Death Line, he was going to pause it. That I was to meet with him, and he uploaded to me the meeting place coordinates.

Off I went.

The two of us hovered over the Great Pyramid of Giza. Below, dozens of tourists snapped photos of the behemoth construction. Several posed so that the world attraction was in the background. Others arranged themselves for the photo so that their index finger looked to be touching the very tip of the pyramid. A British reporter stood before a camera crew that had lined up the Great Pyramid in the background as well.

"Can you see it behind me?" said the reporter. The crew gave him a thumbs-up. "Partially covered, or is it all in? This needs to be right, guys."

The crew suggested he could begin whenever he wished.

"I'm standing only a few hundred metres from the Great Pyramid of Giza in Egypt, where hundreds, if not thousands of people have flocked in recent days. The government of Egypt has issued a formal statement inviting the world to come and witness the first and greatest wonder in the world, or as they put it in their tourism campaign, 'before a year's time is up.' Standing here today, I can tell you that it is truly a site to behold, and I encourage all of you make the trip if you can. From Giza, I'm Roger Thornby. Back to you, Sean."

The camera crew gave thumbs-up once more, and Roger Thornby relaxed his camera face.

The Bookkeeper moved close to me. "I cannot deliver your letter, Luke," he said.

"You don't have the ability, or you won't?" He circled the last option in red marker and sent it back to me.

"Why not?" I said.

"It's a long story. There's a lot of history you aren't aware of."

"What I'm aware of are serious violations going on here, and worse to come. Don't you think it's best to stop it?"

"Best for who?"

"For humanity," I said.

"What is humanity but a vicious cycle of creation and destruction? Take this pyramid right here. I had already been manning the Post-Death Line for a long while when they erected this masterpiece. The ingenuity, the science, the astronomy involved was astounding for the time. The creativity, equally as impressive. I was there to field the thousands of slave deaths associated with the raising of it. In the end, precision, creativity, time, energy, and the cost of human life had resulted one of the future wonders of the world. A stunning landmark for human accomplishment. A beacon for perseverance. Don't you agree, Luke?"

"Yes. It's wonderful."

"Then you should know that I was also around when humans destroyed it, leaving it the maimed version we see here today. A version that spits on the armies of slaves who built it and the Pharaoh Khufu who commissioned it. No slave died for this version," he said, and sent me a before and after version of the Great Pyramid. Certainly the difference was astonishing. The smooth sides made from twenty-ton slabs of polished casing stone had long since been stolen, leaving the maimed and jagged version of today. "For me, it's nothing but the perfect example of creation and destruction — the perfect symbol for the imperfection of the human race. Imperfections, I might add, that before Safia started her work were nowhere near improvement from a biological or generational standpoint. Which brings it all full circle to me and why I cannot send your letter to What's Next. However, to understand my unwillingness to do so, you need to know my story. A story, I might add, that's never been shared with anyone in the Line or with a reintegrated ghost. Please, consider yourself the first," he said.

I sent him a one-thousand-square-foot canvas painted with all ears.

"The story starts with who I really am, which has more to do with who I was before I became the Bookkeeper. If we can agree on anything, we are all a product of our own choices. While alive, I made a terrible one in a fit of rage and turned out to be the first murderer on Earth. Thus, after the murder of my brother, a process had to be created to deal with those who rob the living of their guaranteed time on Earth. Due to my actions, the future of the world was seen. My actions had opened a door to violent thoughts becoming violent crimes, and due to my actions, a process was created whereby the living could cleanse themselves through a return to understanding and regain Required Perspective before passing on to What's Next. That process, as you know it today, is the Post-Death Line. Due to my infamous crime on Earth, upon my death I was sentenced to man the Line for eternity, or until humanity rids itself of the flaws that are responsible for the violent crimes.

"To me, that meant the full extent of eternity, or until humanity wiped itself out through war or the destruction of their atmosphere or habitat. I must admit, selfishly, it is something I have been cheering for. And on a few occasions, you have no idea how close it's come. Nonetheless, humanity carries on, and the chains that bind me to the Post-Death Line, remain. You must understand that, for me, there was no end in sight. And then Safia happened. She managed to slip through the cracks. As you well know, Safia is unlike any RDS to return to Earth. Not only was she wild with anger over her own death, but the lives she had experienced in the Line only seemed to compound that anger. For one reason or another, the Line had done nothing to ease her pain. It had simply failed to provide her Required Perspective.

"Due to this rage, her vibration and energy pattern was different from any and all ghosts before her. Luke, what you saw upon delivery was a difficult ghost with anger issues and lofty aspirations. What I saw was a loaded gun. If she had chosen to go on to What's Next, I couldn't have sent her. Not in the condition she was in. My only option would have been to force her through the Line over and over again until Perspective had been reached. When she stood before me and asked about the condition of her sister, I told her the truth. She was alive at the time. But I also told her what was required to ensure her decision to return to Earth and to live out her lease as a ghost. In the past, I hadn't been so cruel when it came to information of that nature. I would always provide Health Status Conditions of the living attached with the statistical analysis of their odds for survival. This would assist in the decision-making process, say, if a loved one was mortally wounded or had a zero or one or five percent chance of survival.

"In Safia's case, I chose not to attach the statistics or the critical condition of her sister. As I said, I did what was required of me to get her back on Earth. Of course, arriving to witness her sister's final breath was the icing on the cake. This took her anger to a level whereby it would be a dangerous weapon if used correctly. And, as the world knows all too well, it has certainly proven as such. However, you have to understand, prior to Operation Stopgap, she had the power and the intention but lacked the knowledge to harness it. She was the gun with no ammunition, so to speak.

"This is where I come in. I called Safia to the surface of the moon and shared with her some bad news. The conversation surrounded the reality that I would be forced to have her pass through the Post-Death Line for another round or two of Required Perspective. She refused, as I had hoped she would. I revealed that due to her rare and unique anger levels, the vibration patterns that were a byproduct of that intense rage posed a great threat to the living. That, in fact, another round in the Line was absolutely required for the safety of those on Earth. Well, didn't that set her little revolutionary mind to work. Being the precocious ghost that she is, she asked how exactly it was that she could be dangerous. How was she a threat to the living? I replied that that if she were to connect with a living being while enraged, which seemed to charge her vibration pattern, she could potentially harm or kill that individual while attempting to read their thoughts. She promised to do nothing of the sort, that is, if I would change my mind about another journey through the Line. She begged me. Her first experience through the Line, as she described it, was a severe horse-whipping — unbearable and prolonged torture.

"I suggested that perhaps I might be flexible in this regard, so long as she control her anger. So long as she promised to never, ever connect while enraged. She agreed and signed a document to that effect. Contract aside, I knew she would. You see, that was the plan all along. For in that conversation on the surface of the Moon, I spelled out the exact pathway to access her power. I handed her the keys and wished her well. My wish was that she would run wild with the power and act out on her desire to punish and alter humanity. Naturally, it was in my best interest.

"Hours later, the incident in Miami took place. She grew enraged, connected, and ended the assailant's life just as I desperately hoped she would. Instantly, she flooded with fear, since she had interfered with what was meant to be. She sent me a million apology letters. I sent her back the specific rule from the *Handbook* with a further explanation. The truth of the matter is this: the Post-Death Line had been created so that ghosts would not have the desire to change what was meant to be. The Code reads that ghosts are unable to interfere with living things and/or change what was meant to be, but that was written under the assumption that a return to Required Perspective would render them disinterested in doing so. What was lost in translation was that 'unable' really meant 'unwilling.'

"Alas, there has never been another Safia. There has never been someone *willing* to change what was meant to be. The Line had never produced anything like her, nor was there a mandate to deal with her actions or intentions. Technically, there was no firm rule that was being broken. Technically, I was under no obligation to report what was going on to What's Next. The system had failed for the first time, and all I had done was to help foster the unique talents of said individual, post-failure. This was my chance to substantially increase the rate at which humanity improved upon itself. This was my opportunity to shave off thousands of years anchored to the Post-Death Line and finally reach What's Next. Faced with the opportunity, I seized it. Everyone wins. Humanity improves at an accelerated rate, and my sentence as Bookkeeper is dramatically reduced."

"No, you win. Safia thinks she's won. And the innocents lose," I said.

"Innocents die every day. I process the entirety of them."

"You're missing the point," I said.

"You're missing the big picture."

"The big picture is your own self-interest."

"Not according to What's Next, which is desperate to see humanity right itself. Since the day I struck down my own flesh and blood, releasing hate and violence into the world, What's Next has been eager for the humans to return to balance and understanding. To peace."

"I'd like to know why there has been no intervention from What's Next?"

"That's a good question. It's not your fault, but you have little to no perspective on the scope of the Universe. There are simply too many civilizations to monitor, and because of that, there is a process in place. A Messenger is sent by What's Next to visit and assess the civilizations around the universe and report on their progress. Thus, the Messenger, during his whirlwind tour of space, manages to hit Earth once every hundred years to record humanity's population, scientific, and moral growth. During The Messenger's last visit, the world was at war and many millions were dead. The Messenger saw no signs of improvement from the century before and wrote the required briefing to share with What's Next. I signed it, and away he went. So with regard to speeding things up a tad, time was on my side. Safia could complete her plan, her spirit lease would come to maturity, and off she would go to What's Next, long before the Messenger was scheduled to return. Ideally, upon the Messenger's arrival, Safia's work would have returned the world to a state of balance, restored humanity's moral compass, and I would be released. Luke, when you attempt to interfere with that plan, when you attempt to interfere with the fast track to balance, you interfere with my situation as well. Which is why this letter of yours will not be making its way to What's Next. Do you understand?"

"Yes."

"Will you be assisting Safia with Phase Three?"

He sent me a document with two large boxes, one with the world "yes" underneath it, and one with "no." Both of the words were pulsing to the beat of the music from *Jeopardy*, which I thought was both sarcastic and inappropriate given what was required of my decision.

Then the *Jeopardy* music ran out, as it invariably does.

"Please check one," he said.

I added a box that read, "I have a year to decide" and checked that one.

"Choose carefully," he said. "You bought yourself some time to think about it."

26

Catherine Seymour, dressed in nothing but a diaphanous floral dressing gown and worn house slippers, poured herself a cup of tea. This was the teacup with the chip in the rim where traces of gold paint could be found. Throughout the main floor of the house, all of the blinds were drawn tight, but despite that, Catherine could still make out the swarm of media that had set up camp shortly after her historic announcement. She could see the blur that was the city of tents where they had all been living for the past several weeks. Catherine opened a childproof bottle of prescription cough medicine and stirred an ounce or so into her cup of tea. The spoon skipped every time it passed the chip in the rim. *Maybe this teacup is me*, she thought. *Maybe there's a chunk missing of me now. Maybe this spirit, this Safia, maybe she took a chip out of my soul — the good part, where gold used to be.*

She stirred and stirred the prescription cough medicine into the tea as if having concocted a witch's brew of sorts. She wondered if the addition of a dragon scale, eye of newt, and pubic hair of a virgin stirred into the mix might allow her to sleep uninterrupted until the world forgot about Catherine Seymour and her exclusive communication line to the most notorious killer in history. That infamous television appearance — was it a hundred years, or a thousand, or ten thousand? *Wouldn't that be nice*, she thought, *to wake up and be a nobody again.*

She sipped her pain tea.

The clock read 8:59 a.m.

Someone outside, a thirtysomething male with a bullhorn, asked Catherine if she would come out this morning to speak; if she had any more messages to deliver. Seconds passed. Then he asked if she been in touch with the ghost again and if there were any updates to report. Catherine imagined an old Second World War Lancaster flying by her little cottage and dropping a massive payload on the scads of newspeople camped outside. She felt the blast and opened up her blinds to see their bodies disassembled. She imagined the crater on her front lawn and what kind of creative landscaping she might do with that kind of mess. She thought a pond might be nice, since the digging had been done for her. Perhaps with some goldfish in there. *Can't think like that anymore*, she thought. *Not once the year is up.* So she switched up her thinking and went back to the goldfish and how much she liked them.

More than people, these days.

Becoming the most famous person on the planet was not the byproduct she had envisioned. How was she to know that news channels would begin dedicating daily segments geared to every-thing and anything Catherine Seymour? How was she to predict what it might feel like to see her face on every channel — to be picked apart as an angel and devil and everything in between. Catherine looked over to her television and wondered if she should remove the seven iron sticking out of the screen and vacuum up the shards of glass.

It had been three days now since the BBC had insisted on using the most unflattering image of her she had ever seen. The tube had been permanently turned off, and there was nothing she could do about the sharks circling her house. One had even chewed through the phone line in an attempt to force her out into the world for snapshots, even if just to yell and shake a fist. But this cheap tactic did nothing. Catherine wasn't coming out, maybe ever again. She finished her pain tea and felt a half shade of improvement. The courage was once again flowing through her veins, and it was time to get back to writing. Catherine was in the middle of what had the bones to be the greatest trick ever played on humanity. This is what she had written:

> It is with great pleasure that I come to you with another message from the spirit in charge. Given how impressed she is with all of your rigorous efforts to rid your mind of what will constitute Thought Crimes in the near future, she is willing to retool her operation that was set to commence in approximately one year's time. The new rules are as follows: After a Thought Crime enters the mind, every man, woman, and child (over the age of five) is to behave like a barnyard animal to the best of their ability, in public, for one full hour after a Thought Crime violation. The approved barnyard animals are as follows: chickens, cats, dogs, pigs, asses, cows, and ducks. Failure to wholeheartedly emulate one of the approved barnyard animals for the duration of exactly one hour post-Thought Crime is punishable by death. That is all. Now fuck off.

Catherine's unbridled tears of laughter fell to the page and caused the words and letters they hit to become out of focus. She imagined people in all countries of the world burying fists in armpits to form makeshift chicken wings and clucking about wildly, scratching with their feet and pecking at the ground for imaginary seeds. She imagined CEOs of Fortune 500 companies having to kick and bray like donkeys in front of an executive assembly.

She saw streets chock full of human cats meowing, licking their hands, and then cleaning behind their ears, or batting furiously at a piece of trash being thrown around by the wind. Politicians quacking and waddling around legislative buildings. Policemen barking at one another, sniffing assholes, and dragging their rear ends through city parks so as to clean what couldn't be licked.

Based on her suffering with celebrity and the media, this was the kind of joke she wanted to play on Safia and the world. To note, this document also marked the first time she had ever written such a vulgar four-letter word. *What a word*, she thought. *What a glorious word.* Sure, she had thought the word in moments of quiet frustration, but to write it was such a treat. To imagine saying it before a crowd of salivating journalists was electrifying. *That's not like me to say such things*, she thought and blamed it on the codeine, which now had strongly taken hold.

Catherine Seymour held her finished document up in the air, as if it were the Magna Carta or Declaration of Independence. Certainly, it felt like a declaration of her independence, ever since Safia had made a hand puppet of her. Catherine was in the process of taking back the reins, and if this kind of announcement wasn't going to get Safia back in a room with her, she didn't know what would.

"I swear I'll do it!" she cried out toward the ceiling. "You little tart, I'll read it aloud to the nest of vipers out there if you don't come back here and answer some questions! I want to talk to you! How in God's name could you ask something of that nature and never come back?"

. . .

I had been hovering over Catherine's notepad and requested that Safia join us. She appeared, acknowledging my presence with a greeting card. A cheap one. Not decorative. The kind you might find in a dollar store.

"This is torture," I said. "What you are putting her through."

"She agreed to play messenger."

"We need to talk," I said. "I have some news for you."

She sent me a memo asking if I was ready to officially sign up for Phase Three.

"No, it's bigger than that."

"There's nothing bigger than that. And if you're not ready to sign, don't call me back until you are."

And she was gone. A petulant teenager having stormed off to her room.

. . .

Catherine looked down at the message she had written for the media. Would Safia even allow her to read this to the world? Catherine imagined not. She imagined Safia electing to terminate her line of communication rather than allow her precious operation to be mocked. That she would add high treason to her list of reasons to execute someone, and that Catherine Seymour would be the first to fall victim. She imagined the message on the table taking on a life of its own. Lying flat on the antique pine table, the message prodded her into a game of truth or dare. She fully understood the dare, so she opted for truth. The message asked her how she would feel if she accepted the dare and the world saw it for what it was — nothing more than an old woman in the process of going mad?

Catherine crumpled the piece of paper, squeezing it until her arthritic joints ached.

She wouldn't be reading it.

That was final.

However deeply she despised her current situation, being remembered for having lost her marbles was something that her dignity wouldn't allow.

A second cup of tea was poured, and in went the magic potion.

Stir.

Stir.

Stir.

. . .

I called Rob Sutherland to the cottage in Little Bookham and shared with him the interaction I'd had with the Bookkeeper on the surface of the moon. Who he really was and his own predicament.

How he had facilitated the entire thing.

How it was all in his self-interest.

We hovered over a sleeping Catherine Seymour as she snored off that second cup of pain tea.

"Well, good on you, Luke. You sure got to the bottom of it all. But what's the plan?" Rob sent me the image of a picturesque gravel road, heavily wooded on both sides where the century-old maples lining the ditch provided enough canopy to blot out the sun. The sign to the right of it read, "Dead End."

"You're likely right, but let me run this by you. Catherine's crumpled announcement to the media got me thinking. The truth of the matter is this: she has the entire world in the palm of her hand. What if I connected with Catherine and shared with her the backstory to all of this mess? What if she was made aware of the Bookkeeper, and the manipulation of Safia for his own gain?"

"Luke, slow down. That's not wise," he said. I asked him why not, and he suggested that the world wasn't fit for that kind of information — that of Bookkeepers and Messengers and the like. We disagreed on that point.

"It's a long shot, but perhaps Catherine and I can work together to craft the right message to the world. Something that might stop Safia in her tracks or give her pause."

"Luke, what if I told you outright to leave it alone? You wouldn't, would you?"

"Not likely, no. Connecting with Catherine, sharing the truth, and asking for her help to craft a message is likely my best chance to derail this thing. Worst case, people get the whole story before she melts them ... and not just half."

Rob floated around the room a few times. He vibrated and the lights flickered. He was clearly wrestling with something. What I didn't realize was that he was wrestling with my fate, his own fate, and that of the world. Rob moved close to me.

"The problem is, pal ... I can't let you do it," he said. "The Bookkeeper reached out to me and suggested that you might try to come up with a plan to share this information or sabotage the whole thing. He offered me a deal to keep him in the know. I took it, Luke."

I send him the image of a deadpan face.

"Luke, I'm sorry, man. I've been a ghost for too damn long myself, and this is a way out for me, too." Rob grew swollen with vibration energy and uploaded my proposed plan to the Bookkeeper. I sent him a clip of the two of us dressed in eighteenth-century Apache battle attire. In the clip, I was walking away from him, and he pulled a bow and arrow to his cheek and then let the arrow fly. It made its way through my back first, and then my heart. It found a gap between some ribs and the arrowhead presented itself four inches from the meat of my chest. I looked down at it, dripping. Touched the tip of the bloodied arrowhead with my index finger to acknowledge its thorough effort. Then my face hit the cracked earth of the Arizona desert and it drank me in. Rob, in the background, lowered the bow from his cheek.

The Bookkeeper copied me on Rob's Release Agreement, signed and dated at the bottom.

Rob signed and dated as well.

And just like that, my Mentor Spirit was off to What's Next, officially waived of his obligation to fulfill the duration of his ghosting lease.

The Bookkeeper connected with me.

He sent me an image of handcuffs and asked me if I liked the view from space.

27

My half-baked sabotage and Rob Sutherland's betrayal left me imprisoned on the surface of the moon. The Bookkeeper stripped my travel privileges as well as my ability to communicate and connect. No longer could I check in on loved ones and read their thoughts. No longer could I zip from place to place, taking in the best entertainment the world had to offer. No longer could I connect with and communicate with my only remaining outlet for conversation: Safia. Any attempted communications to Earth would simply burn up like a small meteor passing through the atmosphere. Not large enough to serve any purpose.

The surface of moon was my jail cell, my solitary confinement, and it was promised by the Bookkeeper that I would be held there for the remainder of my spirit lease, or until I agreed to help Safia with Phase Three of Operation Stopgap.

Should I happen to revise my position on the subject, I was to reach out to the Bookkeeper to inform him as such. And if released under the promise to assist Safia, I would be forced to remain under her supervision at all times — this to ensure I wouldn't go off and cook up another derailment.

. . .

The first days were spent getting to know my new surroundings. I explored every peak and valley the surface of the moon had to offer. I hovered over the infamous site where Neil Armstrong took his giant leap for mankind and wondered what Armstrong might think of what was going on in the world right now. It didn't matter much what he thought. Not really. I just wondered.

And that was just it.

I had nothing but time and opportunity to wonder.

Wondering became my profession.

I replayed my story with Safia a few hundred thousand times over and over in my head, wondering what I could have said to calm her. Wondering what I could have done to defuse her rage and Operation Stopgap alike. I imagined the scene in Diana's bedroom playing out differently.

One time I let her die.

One time I refused to participate in Operation Stopgap, and Calvin opened fire on everyone, including the baby.

What if I had let Diana die? I kept imagining.

Moreover, would Diana have been willing to die if she knew the full scope of what would befall the world based on her salvation? Would she have demanded that I let her die?

Was I a coward or hero?

Would it have all gone down anyway without my help?

I'd never know.

I hovered on the surface of the moon and watched a massive tropical storm inch toward the Gulf Coast of the United States. Had I the means to travel, I would have instantly visited the houses of locals, preparing for the storm.

The planning.

The boarding up and battening down.

The sense of urgency.

The energy of it all.

Part of me wondered if the best thing for humanity would be for that tropical storm to engulf the entire planet and drop an ocean's worth of precipitation on the continents. Would it be better for them to die by the hand of Mother Nature or a bloodthirsty ghost policing their every thought? Looking to pick them off, one by one, like a sniper from the clouds, until there was no one left? Yes, in my imagination, not a single soul would survive Phase Three.

Stop.

Perhaps I was wrong about humanity.

Perhaps Safia was right, and there were indeed a significant number of individuals on Earth who would successfully change their thought composition going forward in perpetuity. A handful of pure thinkers who would band together, form a community, and push out screaming newborn pure thinkers. If this were the case, many world issues would be solved.

That of overpopulation.

That of pollution.

That of food shortages.

That of fresh water shortages.

That of violent crime.

I imagined this post-apocalyptic world, where the goal of each and every day was to search out and gather pure-thinking survivors. Then breed them.

Search out and gather food for survival.

Share the findings.

Nothing wrapped in cellophane, sitting on a refrigerated shelf with an expiration date slapped on it. Back to the days of having to hunt and kill and leave no waste behind. Back to the days of being grateful for a meal and relishing the gift that is fuelling your young.

Something resembling the animal kingdom once again.

The idea didn't seem like such a bad thing given the state of world before Safia's interference. I wondered if my solitary confinement was getting the better of me, making me negative on the matter, so I moved to the ridge of a different crater that gave me a unnoticeably different perspective on the world. It seemed the only noticeable perspective that was changing was the one in my head.

So I fought it.

As much as I longed to travel the world, I fought it. Somewhere in my spiritual composition, a thread of me knew that the murder of innocents was the wrong choice. Somewhere on the planet, a young boy or girl would be wiped out by a fleeting thought — a young boy or girl who might go on to do great things and solve the problems of the world a different way.

A peaceful way.

I resolved myself to stay strong for that unnamed little girl or boy.

And locked into place my faith in humanity rather than in a gimmick.

28

Many months had passed since I had been jailed and stripped of every ghostly right. For many weeks straight, I hovered above the Sea of Tranquility, where Safia had first brought me, and replayed old stories from the Line. By this point, I had accepted my fate, and my vibration pattern was nothing to speak of.

A frail version of my former self.

Long before, when I stood in front of the Bookkeeper at the end of the Line, he told me there was no such thing as Hell, but my current situation challenged that. When the reruns from the Line grew dull, I turned to watching the digital clock of my spirit lease count down, second by second. I did this for ten weeks straight.

Until Safia showed up.

29

She came to me during the brilliance of a lunar eclipse. From the Sea of Tranquility, she hovered beside me as the burning ring around the Earth exploded out into the darkness.

"The northern lights of space," she said.

I was unable to respond, but thought it looked more like the fires of Hell.

"The Bookkeeper allowed me a visit," she said. "It can't be long."

I wondered why the Bookkeeper would do such a thing. Was it out of pity or a further act of torture — teasing me with interaction for the first time in months? Either way, my fate was sealed. I wished her to go away and never to return. What a wonderful afterlife I had been experiencing before she came into the picture. Before she got ideas in her head and killed a few million people. And then ratcheted it up from there.

"I'm begging that you change your mind, Luke. It was quite harsh when I countered with only one immunity. If you like, I can give you a couple more. If it makes a difference. It was cruel, but you see how passionate I am about this operation. You see how important this work is to me. Now look at you. This is no place for my Colonel. My Colonel is to be by my side," she said and sent me the image of the two gold stars I had been awarded, properly hung in a vacuum-sealed presentation case.

"I am begging you," she said. "Contact the Bookkeeper and join me in the final phase of Stopgap," she said, and hovered beside me until the eclipse had passed.

"Luke, the Bookkeeper has just informed me you haven't sent him anything, so I suppose this is goodbye," she said and vibrated so hard the moon felt as if it might split in half. "So you know, your act of defiance is entirely in vain. I have figured out a way to monitor the Thought Crimes and carry out the executions myself. It's not as slick as our operation would be, nor will it be as fun, but I wanted you to know that I can get it done just the same. More than anything, I just miss you terribly."

Had I the power and ability, I would have vibrated fiercely and sent her back the image of a wall covered with portraits of the greatest villains of all time. An all-star lineup of the most ruthless dictators. The most merciless leaders. On this wall, I had her smiling between Vlad the Impaler and Adolf Hitler.

I just hovered alongside her and enjoyed the image by myself.

"Goodbye, Luke," she said.

Then it was I who missed her terribly.

• • •

Hours later, I concluded that Safia's visit, her one final chance to change my mind or say goodbye, benefited everyone else but me. For the Bookkeeper, especially. He saw me suffer one degree more than I ever thought was possible. For Safia, she got to say goodbye.

Broken spirit that I was, I returned to the comfort of the two digital clocks I had been given. One from the Bookkeeper counting down my spirit lease. The other counting down the commencement of Phase Three.

The seconds, moving like minutes.

The minutes moving like hours.

Months passed. With only two of them remaining before the commencement of Phase Three, the world was facing a purge that would shape the history books until the end of time, if anyone was left to read what had transpired.

What does history matter when we don't learn from it anyway?

Nothing, I concluded.

And nothing was what I could do about the whole thing, trapped on the surface of the moon, slowly drowning in my own guilt and regret.

I recalled the greatest novels I had ever read, the ones that got me through high school. All of the moments wherein there was no way out for the hero; no hope for a battle victory or salvation of the world, the rescuing of a princess, king, or queen. What did these moments have in common? Charts were made in an attempt to batch and analyze the efforts of my fictional heroes, but no concrete data presented itself.

The time for last-ditch efforts and Hail Marys was upon me, but I was lacking two very important ingredients: energy and creativity. The letter I had crafted for the Bookkeeper to deliver to What's Next was read and read a hundred times. Was this letter akin to Catherine Seymour's speech that she had written for the media — for nothing more than the purpose of self-help and to be crumpled into a little paper ball?

Something that Bob the Bully might soak in his mouth for sixty seconds and then fire into the hair of a nearby classmate.

And then it hit me like a bag of light bulbs.

If my attempts to communicate with Earth were to burn up in the atmosphere, perhaps I would focus my energy the other direction: out into the darkness, where a hundred billion brilliant VVS diamonds sparkled in the distance.

The direction of the Messenger.

He was surely out there somewhere making the rounds.

What if I hit him?

So I made a hundred million copies of my thought letter and turned them into a hundred million paper thought airplanes. I fashioned a clip system so that I could quickly load the copies and engineered a mental semi-automatic launcher to speed the process of delivery. The paper thought airplane Gatling gun was then tuned to propel the paper thought airplanes at a speed of a billion times the speed of light.

With every amount of focus, intent, and energy I could muster, these paper thought airplanes ripped out into the universe. Each airplane was given the same intention: to hit the Messenger square in the spiritual composition and to be read.

After the first hour of heavy shooting, my first thought was this: *What if Bob the Bully helped save the world?*

My second thought was this: *What if, like Catherine Seymour, I'm going completely mad?*

30

When Safia's clock approached ten minutes to spare, I broke from the dizzying digital numbers and made my way over to the best vantage point on the moon. Looking down toward the Earth, I wondering how many families had been racked with fear for the last several weeks as the one-year mark approached. Parents doing their best to calm loved ones. Doing their best to pretend everyone in their particular family unit was going to be just fine, as long as they kept their minds clear of Thought Crimes. I imagined two little girls asking their daddy what might happen if they slipped up and thought of violent things. *Will the lady ghost give us a second chance?* they wondered. I had the daddy in my particular fantasy assure them that not a violent thought would ever cross their mind. Why would it? No one could hurt them. There was nothing to be scared of since there were no more monsters roaming the Earth. Then the daddy moved on to a lecture regarding jealousy, and how that was the greatest poison of the day. "For it is only jealousy, envy, and anger that can breed Thought Crimes," the daddy would say. "Which is why we must always be happy with what we have, because what we have is each other, and life."

And the girls would hug their daddy, and the daddy would kiss their faces.

That was my happy version.

The sad make-believe version ended with the daddy finding his two girls in their bedroom, dead and stinking, with a doll between them that had been torn apart due to a tug-of-war gone wrong. The daddy carried the girls one by one into the backyard and laid them side by side on the lawn. He wrapped their bodies in bedsheets and picked flowers from the nearby garden. Flowers the girls had helped to plant. The ones right beside the tomato plants and carrots. He shovelled a hole in his backyard and lowered his little girls down into it.

The eldest first. Then the younger one.

Recalling the best of moments and memories.

The daddy arranged it so that the sisters were holding hands. After doing this, he covered them with a sheet of linen and began tossing the dirt on top of them. Delicately, at first, as if to do no further harm. Upon the last shovelful of dirt, I had the daddy scream up to the Heavens, directly to Safia, demanding that she present herself so that he might attempt to kill her by any means necessary. He swung his shovel violently in the air and toward the clouds, calling her every name under the sun.

And for that, for his murderous thoughts, he dropped dead, according to the rules, and the blood from his nose, eyes, and ears trickled down through the earth, past the freshly shovelled soil and kissed his two girls on the cheeks.

What was I to do but look at the Earth and make up stories?

Happy stories and horror stories.

That's all I had left as the clock broke the ten-minute mark, abandoning an entire digital category along with it.

Moments later, I felt energy move close to me. A foreign vibration pattern I wasn't familiar with. Something that seemed far more advanced than what I was accustomed to.

This was a spirit but bore a different vibration pattern altogether.

"Luke James Stevenson," said the spirit, and I wondered who it could possibly be, since the Bookkeeper's vibration pattern was so easily recognizable. *If only I could reply to this strange force*, I thought.

"You can connect with me, Luke. I have broken the sanctions on your spiritual composition."

"So you can hear me?" I said.

"Loud and clear," said the spirit.

"Who are you?"

"I'm Safia's younger sister, Haadiya Jaffi."

31

I explained to Haadiya that the whole thing had been out of the question, a blindfolded hook shot from half court in which the shooting arm had been broken and badly clawed by a bear.

An effort without a chance. Half a shade better than complete inaction.

I suggested that it was certainly nothing heroic.

"It was done for the salvation of mankind," she said. "Doesn't that make it heroic?"

The fact was this: One of my hundred million letters fired into the universe by my Paper Thought Airplane Gatling Gun was intercepted on the planet Strogmalon. The Messenger was finishing up his report on their progress, and something hit him square in the chest. Upon making contact, my paper thought airplane opened up inside the Messenger's spiritual composition and uploaded the content.

In short, he read it.

"What are the odds of that?" I said, and suggested one in a billion. She uploaded to me the correct odds, punctuating my terrible guesstimate.

"After the letter was read, it was promptly forwarded to What's Next. Which brings us to now," she said, and I sent her over as many question marks as there were paper thought airplanes.

"First of all, on behalf of What's Next, we thank you for the creativity and bravery in sending these letters out into the universe."

"It was the least I could do."

"You understand that, in the process, you have confessed to being a part of an operation that ended lives and interfered with what was meant to be?"

"I do understand and plead guilty," I said. "But the Bookkeeper said that was a glitch in the rules. That technically no violation had occurred." I then shared with Haadiya my encounter with him above the Great Pyramid.

"Nothing but a lie. An intentional misinterpretation. Another part of his plan to get Safia back to work, and you alongside her. The Bookkeeper has failed in his duties and will face further punishment. He is currently being dealt with," she said.

I sent her a thumbs-up but wondered if that was a bit flippant given the gravity of the situation.

"You likely saved a billion or more lives," she said and uploaded to me another medal of honour on behalf of What's Next. That made three for my imaginary vacuum-sealed case, but this one from What's Next was much larger, and technically astounding. Semi-translucent in areas, with rippling iridescent colours coming together to form the text. It now hung beside Safia's Second World War–style medals, complete with old ribbon and sections where rust had set in. Truth be told, I loved them all equally.

"I bet the people of Earth would never believe what saved them," I said.

"How do you mean?"

"A tale that fantastical. A hundred million paper thought airplanes hurled out into the darkness without aim or precision.

Fuelled by nothing but intention. Hitting the Messenger like that.
No one would believe it."

"Humans believe all kinds of fantastical tales," said Haadiya.
"What makes this one so different?"

"I guess that's true," I said.

"Besides, what is a paper thought airplane fuelled by intention
if not a prayer?"

32

We travelled to Safia, who hovered atop the statue of Athena. Her charting and batching system was up and running, and she was now only moments away from carrying out Phase Three of Operation Stopgap. Haadiya approached and hovered close to her.

"Safia," she said. "It's your sister."

"Impossible," said Safia. "You are in What's Next."

"I have Luke here with me, and we want to talk to you," said Haadiya.

"You are not here. This is a trick," and she sent her sister a requisition regarding the confirmation of her identity. Haadiya sent back her spirit number with a certificate of authenticity, complete with an official wax seal from What's Next.

"Of my own accord, I was sent back to deal with this situation that has gone well past out of hand."

"Out of hand? Don't you see what I'm doing, Haadiya?" she said. "I'm making the world a place where what happened to us, where what happened to you, will never happen again. Not if everything goes to plan."

Safia uploaded to her the history of Operation Stopgap and the state of the world since her reign. She attached a feedback questionnaire for her thoughts and suggestions. Haadiya sent it back having filled out only one section. The comments section, in which she wrote the following: *My sweet sister, the jig is up.*

"Safia, I understand what you are attempting to accomplish, but this is not your duty, nor is it the duty of any spirit. You have severely crossed the line," she said, inching forward to her.

"Look at the lives I have saved!" she said. "What about them?"

"You have been a puppet for the Bookkeeper," said Haadiya, "to serve his own purposes." She then demanded of me that I upload to Safia my exchange with the Bookkeeper on the surface of the moon.

She read it ten thousand times plus one.

Safia vibrated with a force unknown to even her. Snow broke from the peak of Mount Olympus and raced down the mountainside, as if to herd the locals into the safety of their homes. Surely, this was it. This was the iconic starter's pistol the world had been waiting for. Sirens rang loudly in the air.

"He took advantage of your rage and mindset and used it for his own good," said Haadiya. "You should never have been allowed to roam the Earth with power like that."

"What do you want, Haadiya?"

"I want you to stand down. I want you to accept your punishment and stop this operation immediately."

"In my future," Safia said, "good girls like you don't die from murder."

"In your future," Haadiya said, "you slaughter millions of good girls like me."

Haadiya promptly sent her all of the thousands of times she had experienced violent thoughts as a child, growing up under the same roof.

"I wouldn't have made it under your law, Safia. And someone else's sister who is as deeply loved is not going to make it under your law either," she said and sent Safia a contract to terminate Operation Stopgap. "You must sign the treaty outlining your surrender, your admission of guilt, and the acceptance of your sentencing before the clock on your operation reaches zero, or you face spiritual decomposition."

"What is that?" said Safia.

"It's the worst fate of all. There is no What's Next in that scenario. No more lives or second chances. There is no more spirit. There is nothing. It all ends. It all goes black for you."

"So whoever presides over What's Next sent you to erase your own sister?"

"No, it was I who asked to be sent."

"To erase me?"

"To reason with you." And then she sent her a billion paper hearts, each of which was folded in the middle and inscribed with a plea to abandon Stopgap and sign the treaty. Signed, "With Love, Your Sister."

"I was afraid that if anyone else was sent, they wouldn't have the patience or give the proper opportunity for you to stand down," said Haadiya. "I did not travel all this way to erase you. I came to save you."

The clock showed twenty seconds remaining.

"What does the punishment look like if I sign? Is the punishment harsh?" said Safia.

"Yes, Safia. It is. But your spirit lives on, and you will reach What's Next in due course or the fullness of time."

Haadiya uploaded to both of us the long-form treaty detailing the sentencing. Safia had been found guilty of the high crimes of Interference and Murder. For her acts, she was sentenced to remain on Earth for the rest of eternity, or until the end of humanity — whichever came first. Moreover, she would be forced to witness the eventual unravelling of her work, to suffer through mankind's return to violence, and bear witness to their long and natural evolution to peace and understanding.

I sent both of them a voice note. In the voice note, a man with a loud bullhorn repeated this over and over: "The punishment is cruel and unusual!" The voice note was three hundred seconds long. As much as I wanted her to accept the deal and survive, it seemed torturous to put her in that situation, especially given the work she had done and her overall mindset. I quickly suggested a plea bargain. In the Line, I had lived the lives of many lawyers and drew on that experience to write up a hundred different plea deals. I selected what I thought were the top ten and sent them over to Haadiya.

"Please consider the following," I said.

"There are no deals to be made, Luke," she said. "Safia, I came because I knew you would make the right decision if I were here with you."

Safia intermittently pulsed with vibrations, and all of the electricity in Athens went down.

"I can't bear witness to what has been proposed," she said. "I don't believe I have it in me."

"Safia, sign the contract!" I said and uploaded to her a giant feather quill and bowl of black ink.

"Sister," Haadiya said, "sign the contract, or I will be forced to proceed with your spiritual decomposition." She uploaded the treaty outlining Safia's surrender, her admission of guilt, and sentencing once again. "Sign it!"

"How am I to make an admission of guilt when I believe I have done the right thing?" said Safia. "How am I to surrender as a murderer of mankind when I have done nothing but save lives and remove the worst of humanity thus far?"

"Time is almost up, sister."

Safia hovered and buzzed.

She flickered and pulsed with intense energy. The unfiltered, chaotic thoughts she shared with me became uncomfortable to accept, and agonizing to bear witness to.

She imagined what the return to violence might look like.

Then ten seconds remained.

She imagined the first act of violence and the state of shock the world would be thrown into.

Then five seconds.

She imagined discourse being traded in for arms. Rhetoric for bullets.

Then four.

She imagined the world wars to come and sitting on the sidelines, unable to do a thing.

Then three.

She imagined the mothers weeping and the shovels digging. The bulldozers piling.

Then two.

She imagined the manipulators becoming leaders and once again turning neighbour against neighbour based on differences of opinion or belief system.

Then one.

Then numbers were something that the massive digital clock had run out of.

"I'm sorry, Haadiya," she said. "I can't accept the terms. Do what you must."

Safia moved toward me and sent over a goodbye card. Inside, the inscription read this: "*To my Colonel, Thank you. I love you. I am sorry. Please don't ever forget my attempt. Safia.*"

I sent her back a stylized heart made of Murano glass falling in slow motion toward a concrete floor. The two surfaces met, and the work of art became a mess of shards and sharp edges.

"I won't forget anything, Safia. And I'll tell your story in What's Next. I promise."

She sent me that simple yellow happy face, and that was the last thing I ever received from her.

Haadiya moved close to Safia and embedded a code in her composition. The code multiplied quickly and began to spread throughout her form. Soon, Safia was covered with the code, and she wriggled and writhed, vibrated and pulsed with everything she had, but the code continued to consume her.

With this, Safia's composition became unstable and loosened. The intense energy, the glue that held her together, snapped with static. Bolts of lightning crashed as her form began the process of breaking apart. Haadiya and I moved farther back as the electrical storm of decomposition took its course.

Then it was over.

Safia was gone.

And spirit code 4495 353 3928 493 9485 was no longer.

33

Haadiya uploaded to me the treaty surrounding my own sentencing. I too had been charged with the high crime of interference. My lesser charge was accomplice to murder.

There was no contest on any of these convictions.

"It was brave of you to send that letter, Luke," she said. "In outing your own involvement and criminal activity, you indeed saved billions of lives. You will be heralded in What's Next."

"In what context?"

"You are a hero who happened to assist in millions of executions. It is a unique situation."

"I didn't intend to be classified a hero."

"Heroes never do," she said.

I read over the harsh sentencing and vibrated with tremendous force. Immediately, I uploaded a formal plea for reconsideration based on my successful effort to prevent Safia's Phase Three from taking place.

"I am sorry, Luke. We are all in agreement that you did a great thing. However, sentencing is final," she said and sent me back a rejection letter with a wax seal from What's Next. There was nothing left to do.

I signed and dated the treaty.

I signed and dated the admission of guilt.

I signed and dated the sentencing agreement.

Haadiya kept the white copy, and she uploaded to me the yellow.

And just like that, I was committed to repaying my debt to What's Next.

. . .

I was never told what happened to the Bookkeeper. Haadiya suggested that his crime, in the eyes of What's Next, for aiding and enabling Safia to carry out Operation Stopgap was far worse than his previous indiscretions. That for a spirit in his position, he had grossly violated a universal law. With regard to what happened to the Bookkeeper, all she said was this: "You will find out in What's Next after your time has been served."

"How long until the world realizes their protection is gone? How long until they go back to slaughtering one another?" I said.

She sent me back a clip of the word "history" spelling itself, the white letters populating in single-second intervals. Then the word disappeared and repeated itself again. Then again.

And again.

And again.

"I hate to agree with you," I said.

Then she was gone.

And so began the next phase of my afterlife.

34

The first spirit for processing approached me. As they all do, she had reached the front of the Line. Number 8585 454 4343 221 5432. At age thirty-three, she had died in a house fire due to her roommate accidentally leaving a collection of candles lit overnight. I offered to connect with her, and she accepted. Based on her spirit number, I uploaded her original Time Card. She downloaded and reviewed it.

"Bookkeeper," she said. "I have a question."

"Based on the fact that you were taken too early," I said.

"Yes. That seems to be the case."

I informed her that, by the actions of another, she had been taken too early and would now face a very important decision.

"Choose wisely," I said.

SPECIAL THANKS TO

The Ontario Arts Council for their development support through the Writers' Reserve Fund; Dundurn Press; Allister Thompson; Shannon Whibbs; my family and closest friends for their ongoing support; and my wife, Kelda Card, for her unflinching belief in this novel from concept to bookcase, and for helping me carve the time to write it.

Available at your favourite bookseller

 DUNDURN

Visit us at
Dundurn.com
@dundurnpress
Facebook.com/dundurnpress
Pinterest.com/dundurnpress